JOAN,

I HOPE YOU ENJOY!!

John A Crowley

6/22/2024

BLACK OCTOBER

BLACK OCTOBER: OFF THE PUSHER

John A. Crawley III

C. H. Fairfax Company, Publishers
Baltimore

BLACK OCTOBER:
OFF THE PUSHER

Copyright © 2010 by John A. Crawley III

All rights reserved. No part of this book may be used or reproduced by any means, graphic, electronic, or mechanical, including photocopying, recording, taping or by any information storage retrieval system without the written permission of the publisher except in the case of brief quotations embodied in critical articles and reviews.

Paul F. Evans, Publisher
C.H. Fairfax Company, Inc.
2901 Druid Park Drive, Suite 205
Baltimore, Maryland 21215
410-728-6421
www.yougetpublished.com
chfairfaxco@hotmail.com

Charles Lowder, Graphic Designer
342 Bloom Street, Suite 201, Baltimore, Maryland 21217
410-978-0399   charleslowder@verizon.net

Because of the dynamic nature of the Internet, any Web addresses or links contained in this book may have changed since publication and may no longer be valid.

ISBN 978-0-935132-33-5 (pbk)

Printed in the United States of America

The characters, all narrative references, and episodes in this book are fictional and are a product solely of the author's imagination. Similarities to any person, living or dead, are purely coincidental. They, and no part of the book, should be interpreted as the author's intent to present an actual representation of past events.

The author's copyright is protected internationally under the terms of the Geneva Convention as revised in Paris in 1971.

CONTENTS

Preface	ix
Chapter One	13
Chapter Two	21
Chapter Three	33
Chapter Four	45
Chapter Five	55
Chapter Six	63
Chapter Seven	71
Chapter Eight	79
Chapter Nine	87
Chapter Ten	99
Chapter Eleven	109
Chapter Twelve	117
Chapter Thirteen	125
Chapter Fourteen	129
Chapter Fifteen	139
Chapter Sixteen	153
Chapter Seventeen	165
Acknowledgments/Dedication	173

Preface

The novel *Black October: Off the Pusher* is set in Baltimore in the 1970's. From one end of this bustling seaport city to the other, to metropolitan Washington, to New York City, there are strong, secretive connections to the emerging urban savagery known as the drug epidemic.

The drug-crazed decade of the Seventies followed the chaotic 1960's. That era, characterized by an unpopular war and government disenchantment, led to accelerated social change, including unprecedented advances in civil and women's rights. These changes rooted themselves in the new decade and into mainstream American life---changing politics, technology, entertainment, and culture worldwide.

In the 1970's, the American population was 205,052,174. Today, it's 310,717,557. Then, life expectancy was approximately 70.8 years, the Dow Jones high was 842, and the low was 669. Federal spending stood at $195.65 billion, and the federal debt stood at $380.9 billion. Today, the national debt is over $13 trillion. Earlier, unemployment stood at 3.5 percent. The cost of a new home averaged $26,600. The median household income was $8,734. Bread cost 24 cents a loaf, a first-class stamp was six cents, and a gallon of regular gas was 36 cents.

Moreover, the Seventies ushered in novelties like the lava lamp, Rubik's cube, mood rings, and pet rocks.

Fads included streaking nude in public, individuals stuffing themselves in telephone booths, and the swallowing of gold fish. Men sported shoulder-length hair, huge Afros, bell-bottom pants, and platform shoes. Women wore everything from ankle-length dresses to halter tops, hot pants, and micro-miniskirts. Bright colors were the rage and the brighter the better.

The decade ushered in Atari's first video game, the Intel microprocessor, MRI's, DNA, and test-tube babies. An American president resigned under threat of impeachment, and a vice president was driven from office in disgrace. Abortion was legalized. Crime and immigration increased. Women, minorities, and gays increasingly demanded full equality. Women bypassed men in college enrollment. The rising divorce rate left an increasing number of women in poverty. Increased numbers of African Americans were elected to Congress, and major cities elected their first African-American mayors.

The 1970's saw the breakup of the Beatles and the death of Elvis Presley. Jimi Hendrix and Janis Joplin died from drug-related causes. The disco age was born. Television came of age. Tabooed subjects and horrors from the frontlines of Vietnam were broadcast into living rooms across America. The television miniseries "Roots" was a commercial bonanza and generated a heightened interest in African-American history and genealogy.

This is the time frame for *Black October: Off the Pusher* and its main characters Trey and Churchill who simply seek the American Dream and hope to love and to enjoy the basics of life. The pursuit of their dream takes a nightmarish detour into the world of drugs and political machinations. At the core of their brotherly relationship are Harlem Avenue in West Baltimore and the group called Black October.

Trey is a bright young man who sees the world unfolding before him. He has a stable family life, advancing education, and love for his teenage sweetheart. His father, a minister known affectionately as the Right Reverend, heads the family. The household also includes Trey's mother, maternal grandmother, sister, and brother living in a two-story, three-bedroom brick row house.

Upon moving to the community, the family's early days are a struggle, but the Right Reverend's work as a stevedore and his budding ministerial duties keep the family fed and housed.

Churchill is the undisputed leader of "The Outlaws," the gang from his Harlem Avenue neighborhood. He is also reputed to be the leader of a vicious citywide gang known as "The Diamonds." Churchill's authority is unquestioned even before he returned from serving on Long-Range Reconnaissance Patrols (LRRP's) in Vietnam. There, he saw the burst of heroin addiction among GI's and knew that tons of raw opium were being processed and shipped to the United States every year. The demand for heroin both in Vietnam and the United States had increased so quickly that the wholesale price for a kilo jumped to $1,780 from $1,240. Once large quantities of heroin became available to American GI's in Vietnam, heroin addiction spread like a plague.

Medical officers discovered that 11.9 percent of the GI's had tried heroin since they went to Vietnam, and 6.6 percent were still using it on a regular basis. In the 1970's, the only way to get high on the five percent pure heroin was to inject it. Today, the average addict is a white, middle-class teenager, and the drug's potency is 50 to 80 percent pure.

Upon Churchill's return from Vietnam, he hopes for a life outside of violence, simply desiring love and peace. Yet, everywhere he turns, the scourge of heroin and death assaults his senses. The drug and its pushers confront and taunt him at every turn, challenging his manhood. If only he could contemplate the video version of his life, and not the snapshot, things could be so different. Into this chaotic period of American history, Black October is born, and Trey and Churchill are pulled into the drug wars on the mean streets of Baltimore.

                                        John A. Crawley III
                                        Baltimore
                                        October, 2010

CHAPTER ONE

"Today I decide my future.
Which path will I choose?

The road less traveled or
the path of least resistance?"

It was a late October day in 1989, and a blustery wind sent a chill up Trey's spine. Or, did the chill come from the sight of the imposing United States District Court on Constitution Avenue in Washington, D.C.?

He wore a dark blue, almost black, pinstriped, three-piece suit. In his new attire, purchased by his father, he could easily have been mistaken for a prominent attorney. The jangle from his handcuffs and the feel of leg irons measuring his steps abruptly cast away the thought.

He looked up at the gray sky and looked down as he felt the crisp wind swirling at his feet. The huge courthouse loomed over him as he tiptoed up the steps. His eyes revolted against the patterns from the gray sky until sunrays danced between the clouds etching patterns onto the front entrance to the courthouse. When a guard pushed him forward, he could only think, *Only in D.C. could life be so beautifully painful.*

As the handcuffs and leg irons were removed, Trey realized this was his long-awaited day in court. A foreboding feeling engulfed him as the court clerk rose and read in an officious tone, "John Archer Ballard III, under indictment numbers 98517445 and 98517446. You are charged with inciting to riot and destruction of property in the commission of a felony."

Trey realized the events at hand are intricately tied to events from many years before. Now, he had to answer to charges from Lorton Reformatory, but the real story started with the Black October murders in Baltimore City. Black October had committed sensational murders for over a decade, but somehow, by some strange series of events, he had been sweep into the abyss.

Trey rubbed his sore and aching wrists as the reading of the indictments faded into his mental background. His thoughts drifted from the courtroom back to 1968. *Yeah*, he recalled. *That's when it all started, right after the assassinations of Dr. Martin Luther King, John F. Kennedy, and Malcolm X.*

"Hmmm," he unconsciously whispered aloud.

Trey grew up on the lower west side of Baltimore City, not far from what would become the gleaming Inner Harbor and the downtown stadiums for the Orioles and Ravens. In his day, the Colts were sports kings. Everyone he knew idolized Colt players Johnny Unitas, Lenny Moore, Gino Marchetti, Mike Curtis, and Jim Parker, the Orioles's Frank Robinson, Boog Powell, Jim Palmer, Brooks Robinson, Paul Blair, and Earl Weaver.

His thoughts drifted back to those pivotal events years earlier that were to have such an impact on his future in a time of care-free and innocent youth.

෴෴෴

When Trey stepped onto the red brick street of Harlem Avenue, Tony quickly appeared from across the street. It was an outlandishly sunny day, and no verbal communication was necessary for the teenagers to convey their mutual desire to spend time emulating their Colts and Orioles heroes. The first order of business, however, was snacks and drinks from Dave's.

Dave's was located on the corner of Edmondson Avenue and Ashburton Street just around the corner from where the teenagers lived. The store was named after its squat Jewish owner. The best friends playfully walked into the tiny grocery store. It reeked of pickle juice, lunch meat, and other strong deli odors. The teens immediately spotted Little Bit loitering in the back and quickly cut each other a wary eye.

Dave immediately admonished the three. "Buy and get out."

Playing it cool, Tony responded, "Thanks Dave. We love you too" and immediately headed for the gumball machine. The machine had as its main prize a shiny, mother-of-pearl handle penknife. The penknife was the envy of all the children in the neighborhood, and Tony put a nickel in every day in hopes of winning the prize.

Unlike Tony and Trey, with no big brother, Little Bit had three older brothers and three underneath him. He used the "pull" from his brothers to back up his newfound gangster persona. He responded fiercely to Dave.

"Look, little Jew man. You Jews think you can talk to us any kinda way. Don't even think you can talk to me like dat."

Tony suddenly squealed with delight.

"Look Trey, look! I got it. I got the knife. I got the knife!" He held the penknife high in the air and jumped so high the blue-tips of his white Jack Purcells pointed directly to the ground.

Little Bit walked from behind Tony and coldly snatched the knife from Tony.

"Thanks!"

The teenagers had grown up together and had been the best of friends, but Little Bit had now chosen to be a gangster. He was cocky and sure, thinking, *Tony had better respect my gangster reputation, my new friends, and the brothers that got my back.*

Wide-eyed and angry, Tony hit Little Bit with a wicked right cross to the jaw. The punch knocked Little Bit through Dave's bread counter, and the knife fell free.

As Tony bent to retrieve it, he quickly realized the potential for retribution and dashed from the store. Little Bit pursued him in a blind rage.

Tony ran in and out between moving and parked cars. Down the street he ran until he made a sharp right onto Harlem Avenue. He made it to his house just in time to close the door.

Pounding on Tony's front door, Little Bit screamed, "Come out you motherfucker! Come out now, or I'll wait and get your sister and mother when they come home."

Neighbors appeared from everywhere watching the scene, but Little Bit would not relent and continued pounding on the door challenging Tony to come out.

Suddenly, to Little Bit's surprise, Tony was at the door, and he saw a straight razor flash in the air. Tony's wide, downward slashing move cut Little Bit down his jaw line, and he fell back in pain, grabbing his face as blood gushed between his fingers. Trey could see the whiteness of Little Bit's teeth through the gaping wound.

Months later, after Little Bit's face healed, he picked up the nickname "Scar" for the three-inch-long, one-half inch-wide scar on the side of his face. The incident triggered an all-out vendetta against Tony.

Thoughts of Tony and Scar evaporated from Trey's mind at the sound of Judge Abrams' shrill voice.

"Mr. Ballard, I understand that you choose to represent yourself in the matter before this court."

"Yes," Trey croaked. He shook his head at the thought that his voice had betrayed him. He had hoped to convey the purposefulness of Angela Davis, the militancy of Rap Brown, and the assuredness of his father. Instead, he thought, *I sound like a cowering, whimpering punk.*

Judge Abrams continued to reprimand. "Mr. Ballard, you will address me as Your Honor."

Trey immediately thought, *Yes, your majesty.* Nevertheless, he gestured and responded cordially, "Yes, Your Honor."

Judge Abrams replied, "Very good, Mr. Ballard. However, it is the duty of this court to inform you that you are entitled to legal representation, and, if you cannot afford it, a representative will be appointed by the court."

A sly smile crossed Trey's lips as he replied, "I think it would be in my best interest to represent myself Your Honor, but I will accept legal consultation."

Focus, Trey, focus. You're in a court of law, and you must represent yourself. Do what you need to do to win. Summon your resources and abilities, and look beyond the immediate.

Thoughts sped through Trey's mind sending him back to Tony and Scar.

A few months after the slashing incident with Scar, the related violence and threats seemed to subside. Tony had managed to come through it without any permanent damage, and he felt safe playing out in the open again.

Then, one day, Trey and Tony were playing football in Evergreen Park, enjoying the sunshine, with a small band of guys from the immediate neighborhood. Trey's team was lined up and readied to let loose its "secret play" when suddenly a cloud crossed in front of the sun, casting a shadow over the field. Trey looked up from scanning the opposing line. He saw more than twenty menacing figures, led by Scar, swagger into positions surrounding the field, obviously intent on advancing on Tony.

With a bleak expression, Trey turned to Tony and said, "I'm not going to let you go down alone."

Fierce accord came from the other guys on the field. "Later for them, Tony. All they do is start trouble all the time. We're just playing football, and look at this."

Fear and exasperation etched Tony's face as he swiveled in his running stance. "Stay out of this, guys. There's too many of them. They want me, and I don't want any of you to get hurt."

The menacing figures raced into the park and tried to tackle Tony. Warm from playing football and strengthened by fear, Tony put on a running exposition that would have made Jim Brown and Gale Sayers proud. He ran through, past, around, and even hurdled tacklers. It was an incredible display of strength, speed, and agility. Finally, he was running up the hill and out of Evergreen Park. Trey and his companions cheered.

The vendetta continued for months and became so bad that Tony approached Trey teary-eyed, saying, "You know man, if I had a brother, I'd want him to be just like you. This battle is something that will only get a lot of people hurt and start divisions involving everybody around here. I'm tired of running and ducking through the shadows and alleys. It's time for me to go. I love you, man." Tony hugged Trey, pushed him back, and quickly spun to leave.

Unbeknown to Trey, Churchill watched the entire scene from a distance. Without warning, he approached Trey wearing a look of brotherly concern.

"Trey, it's never good to see a good friend go away. I've lost a number of good friends, here in Baltimore, and overseas in the war. It's best that Tony go away. Little Bit and his brothers are after him, and they are not going to stop. I don't want to see you dragged into this battle."

"I know you've been looking out for me Church, and you're probably the only reason they haven't been leaning on me."

"You can bet they won't be leaning on you as long as I'm around."

A huge smile creased Trey's face, thinking of having the protection of the most powerful brother in the neighborhood.

Trey awoke from his reminiscence to the judge's sly grin and retort.

"Mr. Ballard, with all due respect to your filings and brief, your desire to represent yourself forces me to state one of the oldest axioms of law. That being any person who represents himself has a fool for a client."

"Thank you for your concern, Your Honor, and I am aware of the axiom, but I stand on my right to due process and, as such," Trey emphasized his last words and let them hang in the air, "insist on my right to defend myself."

The judge tilted her head, and a hint of a smile emerged out of respect for Trey's understanding of the law and his reference to due process. The judge's eyes shifted to the prosecution table and narrowed in what Trey perceived to be a form of contempt for the prosecutor.

During Trey's discourse, the sniveling prosecutor James Gosselin had the look of the cat that swallowed the canary. His mind flooded with thoughts of publicity supporting his political aspirations and an easy victory against a convict stupid enough to represent himself. He laughed, thinking how he agreed with the judge. *Only a fool would represent himself.*

Gosselin would never make the cover of "Gentlemen's Quarterly." He had a skeleton-like appearance with an overly thin face, long neck, and overexposed Adam's apple. Blue veins protruded from under paper-thin pale skin. He tried to dilute his undesirable appearance with classic blue and gray Brooks Brothers suits coordinated with white, heavily starched, thin-collared shirts. Nevertheless, no matter how hard he tried, his Adam's apple would rise and protrude above his collar, and his shoulders would stoop, giving him a humpbacked appearance.

With pleasurable anticipation, he thought, *I'll capitalize on the positives of the trial and drag this out in the media as long as it suits me. I'll be the champion of the people of Virginia. All I have to do is play up the threat of violence from those Lorton savages they export from the District of Columbia and incarcerate in our fair state.*

"This couldn't be any better if I wrote the script myself," he whispered to his second chair. He rubbed his hands together in delight.

This is the perfect time to build my political constituency. I can argue that the District of Columbia is exceeding its sovereign authority by having a federal penitentiary in Virginia. My premise would be that the Lorton facility was not land serving a federal purpose but served the District of Columbia.

I'll argue that the Lorton facility had become burdensome to Virginia, especially to Northern Virginia residents. I'd use the fact that Virginia's state and local police forces provide law enforcement backup to Lorton guards. I'd play on residents' fears of finding their homes invaded and safety jeopardized by porous prison walls.

This case would be the perfect forum. The "Old Lorton Line" would be my ticket to bigger and better things as I crow the "Lorton is your fault" litany.

He almost laughed aloud, thinking that it could glibly be used against almost any opponent at any time. He was on his way. This case would propel him into the limelight.

"Are you ready, Mr. Gosselin?" Judge Abrams barked, her annoyance now obvious. The judge's question and tone awakened Gosselin from his grandiose thoughts.

"Yes, uh, yes, Your Honor."

The bailiff rose and spoke, "In the case of the United States versus John Archer Ballard III, indictment numbers 98517445 and 98517446."

For Trey, the reading of the charges faded deep into the background. Looking at the prosecutor, Trey thought, *Mr. Gosselin doesn't know I'm far from an ignorant convict. This last decade of my incarceration, I've studied every law book at my disposal. Mr. Gosselin doesn't know about Baltimore Polytechnic Institute, Churchill, or the*

Right Reverend. If he thinks this is going to be a cakewalk, he's in for a rude awakening.

An ominous thought crossed Trey's mind. *If I lose this case, I could have decades tacked onto my prison sentence. If I live to serve the full term, I'll be over seventy before I ever see the "bricks" again. Most of my family will be gone, and I'll be a pariah to the rest.*

Trey stood to respond.

"May it please the court. I have received a copy of the indictments and waive the reading. The plea is not guilty to each and every count. I am aware of my right to counsel, and I also choose to waive that right. Thank you, Your Honor."

The judge was obviously impressed with Trey's demeanor and knowledge of court procedures. She nodded her approval with a wry smile. Judge Abrams thought, *I have to respect him for challenging his conviction unlike the others, and I've seen his briefs. They're impressive, thorough, and coherent.*

CHAPTER TWO

"Does my decision really matter?
Or, perhaps, everything is preordained?"

Bearded and with thick, black-rimmed glasses below a huge Afro, Trey bore a stark resemblance to his father. As he surveyed the courtroom, he thought, *I'm going to need luck, knowledge, and all the ability I can muster. I have a lawyer to consult, but I've got to bring out my best. I'll need my angels and my heroes now.*

I must remember the ideas and principles of the great men I admire. Remember Malcolm, Einstein, Gordon Parks, W.E.B., Martin, and so many others. As Gordon Parks said, there is "a choice of weapons," and today's choice is the law. Yesterday's was fire. I must respect the law and understand that I can only control so much of any element.

Remember, Nina Simone, singing and describing Baltimore as the tough town by the sea, explaining the legacy of steelworkers, stevedores, Merchant Marines, and the melting pot of hearty souls they created. I am one such Baltimorean who is here to win no matter the odds stacked against me. The deck is stacked against me, but I have an advantage because I am being underestimated. Take that advantage to a win.

Win. Focus, Trey! Focus. This is when I must leave all childlike thoughts and pretenses behind. Now is the time for me to be a man and all man. There are so many people depending on my success. Win, Trey. Win. To win, I must understand where this all began. Trey paused in thought with his fingers squeezing his bottom lip. *It started on Harlem Avenue with that boy who died in 1970. What was his name?*

෴෴෴

Romeo Mason yawned, stretching his long, sinewy arms above his head and simultaneously arching his neck and back. He kicked off the black covers, feeling the heat of the October sun. He gauged the time as late afternoon and blurted out for no one to hear, "Another day in the office."

He smiled at the thought of his minor empire and the rewards of his profession. Romeo, nicknamed Romy, knew that business was good, and the right palms had been greased to protect him from police raids and interference from rival drug dealers. His only problem was a lack of product, and a telephone call would rectify that. As a seller and user of the product, Romy licked his lips in anticipation of partaking of the new stash. He gloried in the magnificent high from injecting directly into his veins.

Romy awoke from his get-high reminiscences as the call connected.

"Hello," the terse reply came. Now it was time to go into the rehearsed script signifying a drug request.

"My man, need to see ya," Romy blurted out. The script was followed in the usual manner.

"Look I'm busy. Give me a minute to call you back." The telephone went dead in Romy's hands. Romy knew he would get a call back in a matter of minutes, but the call would come from a pay telephone.

The telephone immediately rang.

"What's happening, Romy?" the female voice purred into the line. Romy was caught in a quandary. He needed to know who was calling, and he had to get her off the line.

"Uh, nothing, nothing," Romy stammered. "Look, darling, I got to call ya right back. You home?"

Purring, "Yeah baby, call me right back."

Romy wrinkled his brow, trying to decipher which of his girls was on the line. He pushed the receiver closer to his ear asking, "Whaz that number, babe?"

Anger spilled from the telephone. "What, you don't know my number now? Or don't know who you talking to nigga?"

Shaking his head and slapping himself on the thigh for complicating the situation, Romy took a forceful approach and yelled into the phone.

"Look, call back in twenty minutes" and hung up the telephone. Romy exhaled through quivering lips as the telephone rang again.

Romy's eyes shifted to the ceiling in dread. He exhaled and

answered with trepidation in his voice.

"Uh, hello."

"Romy, that you?" came the masculine reply.

"Yeah, yeah, Connie, it's me," Romy stammered.

"Something wrong?"

"Naw man, just bitch shit."

"You sure, because I can call back?"

Romy's mind swam, *How did I go from a simple telephone call to my connection to this?*

"Naw man, everything cool."

After a moment's silence and some faint uttering, Connie's voice spoke definitively.

"Be in the usual place in thirty minutes." The telephone went dead again.

The telephone rang again. Romy debated answering, and let the telephone ring twice.

"Romy, I'm sorry. It was me, Ramona, who just called."

Romy quickly interjected, "I knew it was you all along. You just caught me at a bad time on a bad connection."

Smiling, he continued.

"Yeah babe, I got a run to make, but I want to see you at my crib in about three hours."

Ramona replied, her manner contrite, "Like I said, baby, I'm sorry, but I just missed you so much. You sure I can't come over now and make it up to you?"

Romy felt in complete control now. He thought of Ramona's beautiful face, luscious body, and accommodating ways.

"Naw babe. Much as I want to get with you, I won't be back here for over two hours. Got work to do."

"Alright baby," Ramona moaned into the telephone. "I promise you won't be disappointed when I come over later. I'll do my apology in person."

Romy smiled from ear to ear. He'd make his pickup, break down the stash, get high, and have Ramona in the next three hours.

"That would be perfect, babe! I gotta run, but I'll see you at the crib in three hours."

Ramona spilled sugar back over the line.

"Okay Romy, I'll see you later."

Ramona waited to hear him hang up and slammed the telephone into the receiver. She had been hearing about Romy and his other women for sometime. She was brought to reality during a confrontation with one of Romy's girlfriends who, worse yet, was pregnant. The girl had cussed her out and threatened to kick her ass if she messed with Romy again. Adding insult to injury, the confrontation transpired within eye and earshot of her mother.

Word of her confrontation with Romy's pregnant girlfriend shot through the neighborhood like wildfire. For weeks, her mother would not let her or anyone else hear the end of the episode. She continued an endless tirade on Romy's morals and asked every day, "Why are you involved with a drug-dealing, lowlife, skinny, sonabitch like Romy?" She was the brunt of jokes from girlfriends and ridicule from her neighbors. Ramona was pissed.

Ramona alternately fixated on love for Romy and wanting to strangle him.

Through clenched teeth, she grunted, "That nigga must think I'm stupid. Who does he think he's playing wit? I'm calling, and he doesn't know who I am. He's probably got that knocked-up bitch over there now."

In her fury, Ramona dug into her purse until she found the crumpled piece of paper with a telephone number scribbled in pencil on it. She dialed the number. Before she realized it, she was venting into the telephone.

As tears streamed down her face, the voice on the other end pleaded, "Don't be upset. You don't need that motherfucker. As fine as you are, nobody should treat you that way. As a matter of fact, where can I find this motherfucker?"

Still feeling the spite, Ramona found herself talking fast, saying she was supposed to meet Romy at his house, but he wasn't home now because he was probably picking up drugs.

"Where's this motherfucker live?" the question angrily shot over the line.

She quickly gave Romy's address and description, adding that she was to meet him in three hours.

An ominous feeling crept over Ramona, and she froze as she listened to the venom spilling from the line.

"Look babe, I'll deal with this motherfucker for you today."

When the telephone line went dead, Ramona looked at the receiver. She felt confused about what had just happened, but she was just so angry. The feeling of dread overtook her again.

What have I done? This guy seems serious. I was thinking he just liked me, but now, I don't know. She slowly hung up the telephone.

The meeting place was Knocko's Pool Hall. Knocko's sat in the middle of the block on Liberty Heights Avenue near Garrison Boulevard.

Romy sighed as he walked down the half flight of uneven, crumbling, gray-painted concrete steps. He stopped inside the dark basement facility to allow his eyes to adjust to the light. He focused on the green felt-covered pool tables dominating the center of the cavernous room. Smoke fumes danced in the low light emanating from the rectangular stained-glass fixtures above each pool table.

Wooden tables with rickety chairs dotted the nooks and crannies at the rear of the pool hall. He could barely see the tables from his vantage point and knew the reverse was true. So Romy took his usual seat at one of the rear tables far from the action. Unknown to most patrons, a rear exit was nearby. With the dim light and convenient rear exit, Romy considered the location perfect for his transactions.

Romy flinched when he saw Connie walk into Knocko's. He had seen Connie in passing but never really met him face to face. Romy found himself preening as if he were meeting Ramona. He laughed at himself, realizing how much he admired and wanted to impress and be like Connie. He loved his obvious power, the drug connections, and the big money he was making in the trade. Mostly, he admired Connie's reputation with the women and the rumors of his many sexual conquests.

Connie sat directly across from Romy, tugging at his ear and rubbing his chin alternately. He stared straight into Romy's eyes as if he were looking for something. Connie remained silent though, waiting for Romy to open the dialogue. Romy was effervescent and greeted Connie warmly.

"Thanks for meeting me, man. I really appreciate you showing up in person."

Connie maintained his unblinking stare, finally saying, "I'm concerned, Romy. Is everything all right?"

"Yeah, Connie, everything's fine."

Connie's eyes shot down as his fingertips tapped the table hard enough to produce audible thumps. When he looked up, Romy could see the flame of annoyance in his eyes. Fear gripped Romy, and he became nervous and fidgety, which caused Connie's stare to become more intense, pronounced, and questioning.

Romy's mind drifted back to his earlier thinking.

How did I go from a simple telephone call to having Connie wondering if I'm compromised? Romy decided to put his cards on the table.

"Look, Connie. Obviously you're mad about our earlier phone call. I was caught up in some stuff with one of my women at the same time you called. Everything may have sounded bad, but everything is cool, really. You know about dealing with these chicks."

"Don't worry about what I know about women."

"Yeah Connie, but I'm telling you it's not a problem," Romy pleaded.

"It better not be, Romy. Look, I'm getting out of here, and a friend of mine will be here in ten minutes. Make sure we don't have a problem, and don't say anything else to me."

Connie immediately got up, spun on his heels, and moved through the dim light, disappearing up the steps leading out of Knocko's.

Feeling stupid and confused, Romy heaved a deep sigh of relief. It seemed an eternity before Connie's emissary sauntered into the room. Even in the near darkness, flecks of light splashed off his gold front teeth. He ambled to Romy's table, ignored the extended hand, and pulled a chair close enough to touch Romy's.

Romy felt a chill run up his back as the man crossed his legs and placed his gold cap on the table. The cap matched the rest of his gold and white ensemble.

The man in gold and white positioned himself to see Romy and everything else in the room. He had the same focused look that Connie had. He finally said, "Look, I'm Goldie, and don't say nothin' right now. I want to see everybody in dis room, and I don't want no shit outta you."

"Hey Goldie, huh, I understand, but I swear it ain't no problem."

"Didn't I just tell you don't say nothin'?" came Goldie's quick, menacing reply.

Starting slowly and enunciating each word, Goldie spoke in no uncertain terms,

"Look, young blood. Da script gits flipped today. I leave and ten minutes later, you on the corner of Liberty and Garrison. Wait there. Any problem?"

"Naw, man, that's fine," Romy replied, trying to keep a smile on his face.

Goldie slowly got up, pulled on his cap, and pimp-walked out of the room.

Romy waited, eyes frequently darting to his watch. After eight minutes, he hurriedly left Knocko's and walked to the designated corner. Ten minutes passed before a black Cadillac Eldorado pulled in front of him, and the door swung open.

"Git in."

Romy initially recoiled but complied when he recognized the face and voice of Goldie.

Romy sank into the soft black leather seat of the Cadillac, and, rather than feeling its comfort, he felt the seat ensnare him. Looking around, he realized the car windows had a dark tint, and seeing inside would be difficult, if not impossible, from the outside. Three men were in the car. Goldie sat to his left, and two men sat in the front looking straight ahead.

"Don't say nothin'," Goldie said succinctly drawing out each word.

The car drove north on Garrison Boulevard and wound its way through urban landscape. The setting changed to a wooded area as the car navigated into Druid Hill Park finally stopping in a secluded area.

Romy's pulse raced and beads of sweat formed over his brow. He silently prayed for deliverance as tears welled in his eyes.

"Strip!" Goldie shouted as soon as the car stopped.

Realizing he had no alternative, Romy slid forward in the cavernous back seat and started taking off his clothes. When he was down to his drawers, socks, and shoes, Goldie patted him down. He searched through Romy's clothes and found a thick envelope full of money. Goldie squeezed the envelope and tossed it to the man in the front passenger seat.

"Count this!"

Goldie continued to search Romy until he was satisfied there was no wire. He threw Romy's clothes back to him.

"Get dressed."

While Romy dressed, Goldie seethed through his gold teeth.

"Look, we ain't got no time for dis kind of shit. Connie ain't having problems with the likes of you. Any mo' problems, I deal wit you. Got it?"

Romy nodded unable to speak.

"Now on, we do things my way. You gave me dat money. I git you da product. You got a problem wit dat?"

"Naw, naw, man. That works for me. I'm telling you man, nothin' was up. I just had a problem with one of my chicks on the phone."

"Sounds like a personal problem to me," Goldie stated flatly. "Now, we got dat package, and we know the money is right. "Right?" Goldie stared with his mouth hanging open.

"Yeah, man, the money is right. I'd never try to rip off Connie."

Romy felt better, thinking he was getting out of this unscathed.

"Look, you git dropped off a couple of blocks from your house cause we know where you live. Another car be along wit your product. From now on, I set up all da connections, and you don't call Connie no mo'. Got it?"

"Goldie, no problem wit me."

The powerful engine of the Eldorado roared to life and slid across the city to Romy's neighborhood. He was dropped off on the corner of Franklintown Road and Edmondson Avenue.

"Git out and wait here."

The door was unlocked electronically. Anxiously, Romy got out, wanting to kiss the pavement beneath his feet, but his feet felt cemented in place. Romy's only concern now was whether he was going to get his product.

Within minutes another car appeared, and the driver gestured for him to get in. A brown-paper wrapped package and an empty brown shopping bag were thrown into his lap. He felt the package to examine its weight and adeptly guided it into the bag. He was dropped off at the corner of Poplar Grove Street and Rayner Avenue. He watched as the car jetted away.

Romy walked south on Rayner Avenue toward Lutheran Hospital. He was elated and relieved that the episode was over but concerned about the product and his future relationship with Connie and Goldie. The drug buy had taken much longer than expected, and dusk was quickly settling. He was five blocks from home and walking fast, but his mind was on drugs and Connie.

Romy was so engrossed in thought that he didn't notice the man's stealthy approach from behind. He jerked in shock as he felt a tap on his shoulder. As soon as he turned, he felt the hard impact of a fist into his solar plexus. The punch was so hard and well placed that Romy immediately doubled over gasping for breath. His lungs begged for oxygen. The agonizing pain that started in his heart shot through every limb of his body, rendering him helpless.

Almost as quickly, he felt the pummeling of two other figures as he was dragged into a nearby alley. The pain inflicted on Romy was the only thing that allowed him to remain conscious. The attack was so quick that it was unlikely that anyone saw what happened.

Romy's eyes blinked as a trickle of oil-covered, filthy water ran by his lips. He noticed the beautiful kaleidoscope of colors on the water created by the oily film. His mind recorded the thought as abnormal to his circumstance. As he pushed his lips away from the dirty water, he felt agonizing pain as he rolled over to face his attackers.

The three faces were contorted with anger and menace toward him. They looked familiar, but he didn't know anyone. He wanted to say something, but the pain from his solar plexus inhibited his speech. Finally, one of the men spoke in a deep baritone.

"You are a despoiler of our women, a drug dealer in this community, and the killer of our children. Your sentence is death."

Romy felt a hard kick to his face, and a small laugh escaped his lips at the irony and absurdity of another inflicted blow. His mind flashed to the equally aberrant thought of the cavalry coming to his rescue.

His rescue and life ended with three sledgehammer thuds from a .45-caliber Colt automatic. He heard the first two shell casings hit the ground as bullets from the silenced, chrome-plated pistol dug into his chest, neck, and temple. Strangely, the last thought that crossed Romy's mind was the distracting telephone call and why it was getting him killed.

ଔଔଔ

Commander Bauer of the Baltimore Police Department didn't often go to murder scenes. He was one step from the top, and everyone knew he was bucking for chief. Mostly they knew he would step on anyone to make it to the top.

A sly grin appeared on his face as he laughed at the color contrast of the dark nipple on the firm, brown breast lying against his bright, white thigh. His thoughts screamed.

I'm leaving this for that little prick Romy who got himself killed.

Arriving on the scene, Bauer sauntered into the alley. His trained eyes immediately verified the reported lack of evidence. Worse, it was nighttime, and little ambient light shone into the alley.

As the cover was removed from the body, Bauer focused his eyes as he methodically examined every inch of the prone figure. He saw the gaping penetration wounds and mentally recorded the use of a high-caliber weapon. He disdainfully threw the cover back over Romy's face.

The bullet casings were gone, if there had been any, showing Bauer that the perps had been meticulous in covering their tracks. Officers had scoured the community but found no witnesses. No one could determine when or why Mason was even there.

No evidence, no brass, no witness, no nothing, as usual. Shit, a voice screamed in Bauer's mind.

He surmised some kind of a drug rip-off, not imagining any of the usual suspects or dealers interfering with someone under his protection.

"Somebody's got to pay," he uttered fiercely in an almost incomprehensible rasp. He shook his head and stalked away.

ఇఴఇ

Connie sat with his legs crossed, tugging at his earlobe and alternately looking at Goldie with a questioning and accusing stare. Goldie was talking fast, his arms flailing in all directions. He recounted all the steps taken to make sure Romy was clean and how he was dropped off with no problem.

"Next thing we hear, the boy's dead, Connie. Nobody seen or heard nothin'. They say its lucky dey even found 'im tonight. If some dude didn't go to take a leak in da alley, da body might still be lyin' there tomorrow. Who knows when dey woulda found it."

Goldie finished his rapid speech with his hands outstretched and his eyes wide.

"Hey Connie, I don't know what happened."

Shaking his head in confusion and disbelief, "One thing I know for damn sure, it wasn't us," he said.

Connie sat back and swung from side to side in his swivel chair. He tugged at his earlobe and rocked his head.

"Hmmm."

He had been extremely uncomfortable since Romy's phone call, and now he suspected that whatever it was that made him nervous might have something to do with the killing. His real concern, though, was any implication that the killing might have to him, or heaven forbid, his connections.

He was on solid ground financially, having already collected the money from Romy, but he couldn't help thinking, *Who ended up with the heroin? Is it going to hit the streets? Is there going to be a threat to me?*

Connie's brow was furrowed in thought.

He shook his head, pursed his lips, and made a smacking sound of annoyance and confusion with his lips and tongue.

Do I need to speak to my people, or should I try to handle this myself?

He had done the stand-up tough play with Romy earlier, which may have been a bad mistake and wasn't his style. He threw his hands in the air in exasperation and clapped them together in an excited manner.

He realized the thought process was getting him nowhere as he blurted out a seemingly disconnected statement:

"If we need to, we'll leave the professional stuff to the professionals. Whewww," Connie sucked air through his teeth and exhaled slowly, shaking his head.

CHAPTER THREE

**"My decision today will mirror the future,
Yet, since most decisions are not fixed,"**

Trey fidgeted on the hard wooden bench as he tried to focus on the preliminary legal matters. No matter how hard he tried, his mind drifted back to Harlem Avenue when he was a kid.

"Trey!" his mother's voice, distinctly and loudly, rang up and down his block of Harlem Avenue.

"Where's that boy?" she yelled out in disgust.

Her eyes narrowed as she shouted to the kids in front of the red brick row house, "If anybody sees Trey, tell him to get home right now!" Her demand was not challenged. When Albertha Ballard spoke, everyone listened. The children immediately leapt to fulfill the dictate.

She surveyed the scene up and down the street, her eyes finally settling on streetlights showing the first flickers of coming to life. Her eyes jetted to the white marble steps on which she stood. Close scrutiny showed a small black scruff mark on the gleaming white steps. She mumbled to herself, "That boy was supposed to scrub these steps, and he's nowhere to be found." Angrily, she spun on her heels and was inside the house, disappearing as quickly as she had appeared.

Trey's mother's stern voice reflected both her concern and resentment for Trey's violation of the rules. She was a matron of the church who demanded and received respect wherever her foot fell. The rule of the Harlem Avenue quadrant was that children be at home or on their steps when the streetlights came on at dusk. Miss Albertha, as she was commonly referred to, was strict about the rule. She was so strict that the neighborhood joke was, if Trey were not at home when the streetlights came on, he'd run home breaking them all the way, so his mother wouldn't see them.

Like African drums from another time, Trey's mother's message resonated far and near to be picked up and transmitted over greater distances. Unlike the African drums, the message was carried by word of mouth from the red brick streets of Harlem Avenue and Claymont to the black asphalt streets of Ashburton, Edmondson and beyond.

Trey's block of Harlem Avenue was four blocks from Poplar Grove Street and two blocks west of Lutheran Hospital off of Ashburton. The hospital had an amazing emergency dispatch time to the neighborhood. Often, hours passed before an ambulance would arrive to treat or to remove the numerous injured parties. The neighborhood joke suggested that it would be better to drag yourself to the hospital rather than wait for an ambulance.

Miss Albertha's message was transformed by the time it reached Trey's ears, just like the old game of whispering something in your neighbor's ear and passing it in a circle. When it reached Trey's ears, he heard, "Oh Trey, you're in trouble. Miss Albertha's been calling you, and she says she's going to beat your butt." Making matters worse, Trey was already in dire straits.

One game Trey and his friends created was called the "Edmondson Avenue Trolley Race." A trolley car ran east and west on Edmondson Avenue into and out of downtown Baltimore. The first stop in Trey's neighborhood was at the corner of Edmondson Avenue and Ashburton Street. The second stop was at the bottom of the hill, a distance of five blocks. The sidewalk was uninterrupted from start to finish as this stretch ran along Evergreen Park.

Trey and his compatriots used their wagons to race the trolley down the hill in a competition that included the trolley driver and passengers. The race started once all the passengers were boarded and seated. The driver would eye the wagon, and there was a silent signal to start.

One kid would push the wagon to gain momentum, and a second would guide the wagon. The pusher would get a running start and jump in behind the driver. This day it was Trey's turn to push the wagon, and he was determined to get a good start before jumping inside. As the trolley started its descent of the hill, Trey ran and pushed the wagon as fast and hard as he could. However, just as he was about to leap into the wagon, he tripped. He was so focused on winning that he didn't release his firm grip on the back edge of the wagon and was dragged down the sidewalk, skinning his knees and generating enough friction to drag off his pants.

Realizing he had lost his pants, he let go of the wagon and raced back up the hill in his underwear. He hurriedly pulled his pants on, but all who had witnessed the event laughed uncontrollably. Trey could only imagine how funny it was for the trolley driver and passengers. They probably laughed all the way to downtown Baltimore. Worse still, he now had to face his mother for a violation of the rules. He raced home while fastening his belt and looking at his bloody knees.

Trey's Harlem Avenue nurturing grounds were segmented into territories. A particular street or four-block square represented a neighborhood. Trey's neighborhood was a paradox for him. It was beautiful, and it was great fun but also potentially very dangerous.

Some of the neighborhoods competed against each other in sports and some as gangs. "The Outlaws" operated from Trey's Ashburton Street, Harlem, Claymont, and Edmondson avenues quadrant. The undisputed leader was Churchill. Trey never knew whether this was his first or last name. Nevertheless, his presence was so commanding that he didn't need a second name, just like Magic or the Babe. One name and you knew him.

Trey was in the unenviable position of being a small kid with no big brother until Churchill took him under his wing. Without Churchill, Trey could easily be intimidated and victimized by the older, tougher, streetwise neighborhood bullies. Trey needed and wanted Churchill's guidance, instruction, and protection, and he thanked God that he'd been adopted as Churchill's street brother.

Churchill's authority was unquestioned and undisputed in the 'hood, and he was reputed to be king of the citywide gang known as "The Diamonds." Feared throughout Baltimore, "The Diamonds" gained notoriety for leaving pieces of cut glass in the foreheads of their victims. Rarely was any group feared throughout Baltimore, but tales of "The Diamonds'" exploits reverberated across the city.

The older guys in Trey's neighborhood owned no weights and had no gyms or spas where they could work out. Instead, they did weight repetitions with manhole covers to build their huge muscles. Trey often fantasized about having the tremendous muscles of the older guys. The only time Trey recalled seeing a bench press and weights was a day in Evergreen Park. Two guys from a different neighborhood were lifting weights on the bench press when one guy decided to step aside and urinate in the open. Trey was with a group of kids playing in the area when Churchill walked up to the man and hit him so hard he knocked him out with his penis still in his hand. Churchill glared at his companion and fiercely blurted, "He shouldn't be exposing himself in front of all these kids." Churchill was a real hero to the little people in the 'hood.

Another time a large, angry dog terrorized the children in Evergreen Park. No one knew where it had come from or how to get rid of it. Once Churchill became aware of the problem, he stood vigil. When he saw the dog, he immediately confronted it. The creature ran and lunged for Churchill's throat. One swift pincer move snapped the dog's neck between Churchill's powerful forearms. Trey heard the sickening yelp of the creature as it fell to the ground. When things calmed down, it was hard to imagine that the creature had been a menace to anyone.

Trey's job as a junior "Outlaw" and Churchill's adopted brother was to be a set-up man. If a well-dressed guy wandered in the vicinity of the 'hood, Trey would approach him and demand money in a threatening tone. Typically, the guy would collar and berate him or start to beat him up, signaling Churchill. He would appear seemingly from nowhere, fiercely questioning, "Why are you messing with my little brother?" Even though Churchill didn't need help, in seconds more "Outlaws" would appear, and they would beat and relieve the victim of his money, jewelry, and clothes. Trey saw many a guy running up Edmondson Avenue in his drawers.

Being from a church-oriented family, Trey felt he was the only family member who understood the mores of the street. Trey loved his family and his father, nicknamed the Right Reverend. His father constantly preached the importance of family relationships and values.

Trey's household consisted of his mother, father, maternal grandmother, sister, and brother, all living in a two-story, three-bedroom brick row house. Trey shared a room with his younger brother, Clifton. His sister Brenda and his beloved Grandma Emma shared a room.

The early days were a struggle for the family. The Right Reverend's work as a stevedore started in the afternoon and lasted until late at night. His mother's work required her to leave early, and she didn't get home from work until after six o'clock. His grandmother was the perfect bridge between their schedules, and her labor of love was the children.

Grandma Emma was the only grandparent Trey had ever known. She and his mother had moved to Baltimore from South Carolina when his mother was only six. They had struggled for years with his grandmother working as a domestic. Using her great cooking ability and taking in laundry, she made ends meet. She had once been a highly sought cook in the resort town of Myrtle Beach, South Carolina even though she was born in Sumter.

There was a deep love and attachment between Trey and his grandmother. They were virtually inseparable, and Trey was highly protective of her. Although Trey never particularly cared for Sunday school or church, he was up early every Sunday morning, dressed, and seated by the front door waiting for his grandmother. They would trek across the city to her church in East Baltimore. Trey would never let his grandmother take the trip alone.

Trey's Grandma Emma taught him his first lessons in fighting, instructing him, "Keep up your guards, and the first chance you get, hit 'em in the eye. If they can't see ya, they can't beat ya." And so it was. Even though Trey was small and skinny, he gained a reputation for being feisty and delivering blows that would stick and tell.

To Trey, Grandma Emma was a black beauty. She seemed to be made of sinew and black twisted muscle on a rail-thin body

Her obvious great strength had come from years of cleaning homes, cooking, and taking in laundry. This contrasted with her gentle eyes and soft-spoken manner. Trey's mother and grandmother were dark-complexioned beauties with flat noses and thick lips. The Right Reverend was light-skinned, leaving Trey with an almost bronze-orange complexion. Trey loved summer because, in short order, the sun would push his skin tone closer to that of his beloved grandma and mother.

Trey remembered the day he first saw Grandma Emma cry. It started when the issue of discrimination was introduced to his young, fertile mind.

"Negroes are not allowed to go to certain places in the city." Knowing that Grandma Emma was a great joker, Trey laughed.

"Stop Grandma. It's crazy for anyone to do anything like that." Grandma Emma's eyes filled with tears, and suddenly Trey knew she was not joking.

Although Trey could see that it upset his grandma, he wanted to understand and to make sense of it all. Grandma Emma tried to explain that because Negroes were of darker complexions, they were not permitted in certain restaurants, movies, and other places, but Trey was having a hard time comprehending. *How could anything like this be real?*

Many of the things that agitated his father began to make sense to him now, and Trey began to feel agitated too. *This was important. It was important enough to make his father bear the weight of it while also trying to change it. It was important enough to make his grandma need to talk about it even though it made her sad.* Trey made a promise to himself that day that anyone who made his grandma cry would have to answer to him.

Trey had grown up as part of the street culture, and any neighborhood threats against his family were conveyed directly to him.

"Tell your father that we were getting ready to jump him last night. He's a minister, but he don't need to be out here late at night like that."

How could he tell his father and protector that he was being threatened?

Trey's father was far from helpless, however, and had developed a reputation as a person not to be trifled with. On one occasion, Trey was trapped on top of a car with two vicious dogs leaping and snapping at him. His Aunt Margaret, who lived on Claymont Avenue just across an alley from the Ballards, saw Trey's predicament and immediately called his father. Seconds later, the Right Reverend was on the scene with his double-barreled shotgun on his shoulder.

With a smile on his face, and in a very low tone, he said, "I've always loved to hunt." The dogs were quickly led away.

Harlem Avenue wasn't all about fighting, gangs, drugs, and violence. Although Trey recalled those days with a certain amount of despair and uneasiness, he also recalled many good times. His home had a door that was open to many visitors. Parishioners, neighbors, and friends were constantly in and out the door. Trey's older sister had virtually adopted Aunt Margaret's daughter, Vikki, and consequently she grew up as Trey's sister. From this alliance, the Ballard house had become the de facto playground for the neighborhood girls. Trey had no choice but to endure evenings at home with the girls.

Perhaps that, more than anything, led Trey to spend his days on the street roughhousing with the boys. Still, listening to the girls' experiences gave Trey his understanding of why guys and girls have relationship woes. To Trey, it was all so very simple; girls were not that different from guys. They were the same: smart or dumb, cute or ugly, fat or skinny or even super tough. Unfortunately, too many people tended to look at the physical attributes of people, rather than the things that really counted like character, maturity, perceptiveness, and integrity. *People look at each other in snapshots,* he thought, *and not as long-running movies: pretty stupid indeed.*

Whenever something happened in the 'hood, Trey's parents would send him out to find the facts. A youngster in the 'hood was generally ignored and virtually invisible in big crowds. At times, this would allow Trey to go out after dark. He always took more time than required for his reporting, and his mother eyed him suspiciously upon each return. However, he was a reliable reporter capable of dissecting the event, providing insight, and identifying all parties involved.

One of his more memorable reporting jobs happened early one afternoon when the neighborhood was sleepy and quiet. On a burning hot summer's day, Trey walked home from playing baseball in Evergreen Park. He noticed a stranger on Claymont Avenue walking toward him and taking off his clothes. He had apparently just gotten off of the trolley on Edmondson Avenue. In short order, the man was naked, except for his fedora.

The naked man approached and then tried to become amorous with a teenage girl named Sandy, one of the great beauties in the neighborhood, a true ghetto flower. It wasn't long before her brother Gus and boyfriend Midge heard Sandy's pleas and rushed to her rescue.

After the man took a savage beating from Midge and Gus, Baltimore's finest came on the scene. Sirens blared from squad cars trailed by a paddy wagon. With true genius, the officers pushed the naked man against a wall and then spread his arms and legs wide to make him assume the position. Obviously, there was nowhere to search but under his hat, which Midge and Gus had earlier knocked off.

After frisking him, the officers spun the suspect around to face them. With his penis dangling in front of him, he started urinating on all of the policemen. The assembled crowd roared with laughter. The officers, one holding each limb, except for the flowing penis, flung the naked man into the back of the paddy wagon. The officers were reminiscent of the Keystone Kops stumbling over each other with nightsticks raised high trying to get to him. Trey couldn't wait to report the events to any member of the family willing to listen. As Trey's cousin said years later, "I thought you would grow up and become a journalist."

The naked man incident was the news on Harlem Avenue for many months and was recounted with humor and curiosity time after time. Everyone wondered why someone would disrobe publicly, and the discussion always came back to the action of the police. They laughed at the foolish frisking of a naked man and the ultimate humiliation of being urinated on but recoiled at the savage beating of the man. Yet, this incident was to become a distant memory due to events playing out in the neighborhood.

Poplar Grove Street was four blocks east of where Trey lived on Harlem Avenue. Although a short distance away, it was a neighborhood distinct from Trey's. Most people in one area did not interact with or even know people in the other.

One night at nine o'clock, Trey was rousted from his studies by the Right Reverend.

"Trey, something's going on up by Poplar Grove and Harlem. Go check it out, and let us know what's happening." Trey donned his light jacket, scurried down the steps, and was quickly out the door.

Looking west on Harlem Avenue, he saw the flashing lights of fire engines and police cars. He immediately dashed toward the lights. He chuckled as he ran, loving the freedom of the night and anticipating hanging out with his buddies before going home with his report.

As he approached what appeared to be a row house fire, he realized something was different. It was an Autumn night, temperature in the mid-sixties, which would mean there was no need of a stove for warmth or some other form of heating that could spark a fire. The faces in the crowd reflected dread, shock, and anger.

What was going on?

He filtered through the crowd picking up thoughts. As usual, he was able to sidle up to people engaged in conversation. In no time, he gleaned that someone had died under suspicious circumstances.

Trey again sidled up to a group that seemed very verbose and particularly angry.

"It's a damned shame!" a man blurted out. "That woman been trying for months to keep them damn drug dealers off her steps and now look at this shit."

Tears streamed down a woman's face.

"She cussed 'em and threw water on 'em to move down da

block, and what dey do, throw a rock through her window. She called the police all da time, but dey didn't do a damn thing. Dey don't give a damn about around here. I bet if dem damn drug dealers were up on Reisterstown Road, the police would know what to do den."

Flames twisted into clouds of thick, black smoke that were sucked into the night. The smell seemed different from other fires Trey had witnessed, and the crowd seemed more restless. He continued to filter through the crowd until he saw Churchill with his homeboys. Again, he was transparent to everyone except Churchill who cut him a wary eye.

Churchill had a grave and stern look on his face as he spoke.

"Man I ain't seen nothing like this since 'Nam. It's a terrible thing to have to smell burning bodies in your own neighborhood. Who the hell do these fucking dealers think they are?"

"Ya know, we don't even know how many people was in there, but for damn sure whoever's in there didn't make it," another man interjected.

"Yeah man," Churchill continued icily. "When I got here, flames were coming out of the second- and third-story windows, and it was so hot that you couldn't get within twenty feet of the house. Whatever they threw in that house created a fireball."

Another angry voice flared. "That woman supported herself and three sons, never bothering nobody! These shit-ass drug dealers felt like they could push her around. If a real man was there, this never would have happened."

Bowing his head in obvious anger and disgust, Churchill continued slowly.

"You know we put our time in the 'Nam, and we come back to this shit. I'm working to be the best person I can be. How am I supposed to let these street punks run around here and do whatever they want? What if the police can't or won't do anything? Am I supposed to ignore this shit until they come after me? I tell ya what, let one of dem motherfuckers get me wrong. I'll be LRRP-ing again, and I know damn well they won't like that." Silent acknowledgment in the forms of nods and daps from the other men cemented the statement.

Trey had heard the brothers speak of LRRPs before. He understood that LRRP stood for "Long-Range Reconnaissance Patrols." They were soldiers who pretty much went into the Vietnam jungle and killed as much and as indiscriminately as possible and then reported back to the base.

Trey felt that he had the information he needed to retreat home, but this time his journalistic enthusiasm was tempered. In short order, Trey had gotten a flood of information, experiences, and sentiment, which had not quite been distilled within his mind.

He slowly filtered his way out of the crowd and headed down Harlem Avenue, taking one last look over his shoulder, shaking his head in resignation and disgust. He detected moisture in his eyes then, not realizing that he had started to cry. A lonely hot tear streamed down the side of his face, and he hurriedly wiped it away, hoping no one had noticed. He had forgotten he was still invisible to the crowd and was not the only person in tears.

Having run up the street, he now found himself slowly walking home, his feet now lead with shock. He forgot about taking advantage of his late evening freedom and felt sorry that his father had asked him to witness this tragedy. When he finally walked in the door of his house, the entire family had gathered to get the news report, excitement registering on their faces. The Right Reverend saw Trey's sullen face, and he immediately ushered everyone out of the front room, quickly returning to hug Trey close.

"I love you, son."

Guiding Trey into the chair usually reserved for him, the Right Reverend gently said, "Whatever happened up there has obviously upset you, and I feel terrible for putting you in a position to see something that you shouldn't have. Now, if you don't want to talk about it, that's fine, and I'll go find out what happened myself."

Looking up at his father with tears flowing unchecked, Trey responded. "Dad, something bad happened. They may need a minister."

Trey would never forget the look on his father's face at that moment. It seemed to convey so many things at the same time, compassion, love, concern, dread, and anger. The Right Reverend fought for control.

"Bertha, please get this boy some hot chocolate, and get him in bed. I'll be right back."

The next morning it was splashed all over the newspaper:

"Drug Argument Ends in Tragic Deaths" in large, bold letters that seemed to shout the news.

In the 'hood, the familiar African drums came back to life. While the paper carried pictures of the slain family along with pictures of firefighters removing the family members in body bags, the drums carried a warning of retribution. Everyone could feel that something was in the air.

The world had changed forever.

CHAPTER FOUR

> "My destiny is predicated at the point of decision,
> And secured every day,
> And every moment the path is chosen."

The courtroom buzzed as the trial's preliminaries ground to an end. Trey gauged his surroundings as he tried to relax and appear confident. He knew he was in for both a battle and test of wills against the prosecutor. Biting his nails, Trey's mind drifted to questions of power and response.

He thought, *Oftentimes in wars and struggles for power, an innocuous event or a particular injustice is the catalyst for great change. The Texans could remember the Alamo, the Nazis used the Jews, and the Boers focused on the mealies. The final straw for blacks' war on drugs was Mario Puzo's "The Godfather." In the best-selling novel, the Mafia saw no problem selling drugs "To the niggers because they don't have souls anyway." Puzo hadn't heard James Brown when he told everyone, "We've got soul and we're superbad!"*

The brothers in Baltimore had finally had enough. A radical and clandestine group started making its presence known with graffiti. Trey remembered the phrase "Black October, Off the Pusher" cropping up on walls all over town. The graffiti's proliferation coincided with the deaths of heroin dealers. It was not unusual that a drug dealer would get killed in Baltimore, but the Black October killings were different. Written warnings were discovered beside the bodies, including, "These parasites are selling death to the black community" and "Off the Pusher."

The police didn't know or seem to care about Black October. Much like "The Diamonds," it existed, but you didn't know who was behind it. The night of the fire, the family's lost lives and the statements about retaliation popped into Trey's mind.

He recalled these strange doings coinciding with the brothers going and coming back from Vietnam. His surrogate brother Churchill had been drafted and served in the war. He was silent and brooding after his return, and his mood seemed to be getting progressively worse. Trey noticed that everyone except Churchill's war friends cut him a wide berth. He was angry and solemn. When Churchill was angry, no one crossed his path.

Trey thought about Vietnam and the testament to the 'hood that no one from the Harlem Avenue quadrant was ever killed. Many of the guys from the 'hood bragged that Vietnam was the best vacation they'd ever had. All the drugs, girls, and liquor you wanted and could afford were there. They talked about getting high smoking marijuana, hashish, and opium. If they weren't fighting or LRRPing, they were drinking, getting high, and heading to Mama San's for entertainment.

They often commented that the service even threw in three hots, a cot, and a paycheck. They were given excellent weapons and a license to kill as they joined a cadre of homeboys from New York, Chicago, Philadelphia, Detroit, D.C., and beyond they could really count on.

The brothers from the 'hood never enlisted but found themselves in the military through the draft. None entered as officers or had any idea about a deferment, conscientious objector status, or going to Canada to avoid the draft. They reported, did their basic training, and went directly to Vietnam. They served their tours and came back to the 'hood as unemployed drug users and trained killers.

The brothers' assignments were rarely in support roles. Instead, they were typically LRRP's. In many ways, their stories about Vietnam sounded better than being in the 'hood. Trey had thought about going to Vietnam. He knew he was as tough as some of the returning veterans, and he wasn't opposed to proving it. The guys were older and larger, but he accounted himself well against them in sports and fisticuffs.

A former storefront church overlooking Evergreen Park now served as the 'hood's gathering spot. It had a long, partially hidden porch and steep steps long and wide enough for large groups to sit on and to play cards, to joke, and to drink. Here, Trey listened to Vietnam War veterans and noticed the changing of their tunes after being home awhile. The vets were happy and filled with excitement for the future after their return from Vietnam. In time, their rhetoric changed totally.

Trey recalled Churchill's protestations:

"I leave and go fight for my country, and what do I find when I come back? The same old shit! I can't get a decent job. Niggers strung out on that damn heroin stealing everything not nailed down. Motherfucking white man thinking I'm still gonna kiss his ass. He must be fucking crazy!"

Now, the glamour of the war was lost for Trey.

"Look at this shit! Vernon Jordan's article hits it right on the motherfucking head." Churchill paraphrased Jordan.

"Listen. It's always the black veteran who gets the short end of the stick after coming back to the world. Ain't that the motherfucking truth!" Churchill shook the paper to straighten it out and looked at his comrades for encouragement. His head moved from side to side in the negative while a sour expression was fixed on his face.

"Look, he says that now we back, the statistics say we unemployed more than twice the rate of other veterans."

Butch interjected.

"Time to send a frag up somebody's ass, I say," and then he took several deep swallows from the green Thunderbird bottle. Churchill watched Butch's Adam's apple bob with each gulp and wondered how he could stomach wine that smelled so bad. Butch and Churchill had been homeboys as long as Trey could remember, and, from what he understood, they had served together in Vietnam. Butch's reference to fragging related to a number of incidents in Vietnam in which soldiers had thrown fragmentation grenades to kill or to maim superior officers whom they hated or felt would get them killed.

Churchill cut a menacing look at Butch followed by a conciliatory smile. Butch gave Churchill the power sign, showing a raised, tightened fist and passed him the Thunderbird. He took a small sip from the bottle and passed it to the next homeboy. He belched and started again.

"All right, all right, let me finish. He says they don't count people who ain't looking for work, meaning up to four times as many black vets are unemployed. I guess we ain't the only ones who gave up looking, huh? Worse, he says that lots of black GI's get dishonorable discharges for stuff that white soldiers get off for scot-free. Shit! We're getting fucked going and coming."

"Yeah," interjected Butch. "Just goes to show you like I always say, frag 'em and forget 'em."

Churchill continued slowly and more thoughtfully.

"The story goes on to say that even if our records are clean, the military uses a special number system on discharges, with codes that give secret information. I bet those codes keep us from getting government jobs and sweet gigs like Bethlehem Steel, the Post Office, and General Motors."

Shaking his head, he looked at Butch, saying sarcastically, "Yeah Butch, I bet dey got a code on your discharge papers." The vets laughed in unison, slapping each other with high fives and going into complicated hand daps.

"Damn skippy!" Butch responded.

"Listen, listen, I'm almost finished," Churchill begged. "This Vernon Jordan knows what he's talking about. He says our civil rights have been violated and that the coding practice should end immediately, and a massive public employment drive should open to get us decent jobs at decent salaries." Churchill finished reading and tossed the paper to Butch.

Butch spoke while pretending to read.

"Ya see. Dat's what I'm talking about. I'm definitely an angry veteran, and I'm definitely tired of dis bullshit going down on da streets. Somethin's got tah give, and it ain't gonna be me. Believe that shit."

Another angry vet blurted out, "Now these sons-of-bitches are using the corpses in body bags to ship that shit over here. It's genocide, pure and simple. Yeah, I heard about the drug scheme where they're sewing heroin into the bodies coming from Vietnam. Wanta bet on the color of the corpses?"

The next day, the police raided a house just north of the Harlem Avenue quadrant. Trey assumed his journalist role and rushed to the scene. After the police broke down the front door, six adults and ten kids were led from the row house. *It's funny*, Trey recalled, *I didn't know any of the kids.* The police not only recovered a large amount of cocaine but uncut heroin, money, and guns.

When the main culprits were led out in handcuffs, he heard Butch say, "We should be fragging these motherfuckers for selling that shit in our neighborhood." A low murmur of agreement was accorded his statement.

Churchill seemed particularly angry and gave a nod to his homeboys. He spun on his heels to leave. Knowing this was a sign that he was deeply troubled, his homeboys knew he was not talking anymore.

Trey recalled, *I never heard Churchill talk as much as he did the day he read from the Vernon Jordan article.*

Churchill dejectedly walked with his head bowed and soon arrived at Ramona's house.

She welcomed him, and her mother smiled her approval on seeing him. Soon he and Ramona were alone in the basement of the house. Since the death of Romy, Churchill and Ramona had become constant companions, and love was blooming. She had quickly forgotten her infatuation with Romy and now found the attention of Churchill far more satisfying.

Churchill was the complete antithesis of Romy. He was muscular, tall, and handsome in a rugged man's man way. He was not boisterous or flamboyant. When he dressed to go out, he was "as clean as the Board of Health" but never flashy, even choosing not to wear jewelry. He was the kind of man whose very presence demanded attention.

Ramona threw herself into Churchill's powerful arms and was rewarded with a light peck on her lips. Her head jerked back in surprise, knowing the depth of the feelings that had grown between them as well as Churchill's insatiable desire for her.

"Church," she squealed, "What's wrong?"

Ramona fell back a step when Churchill released his embrace. Concern gripped her, and heat rushed to her eyes.

"Church, what is it?"

Churchill plopped onto the green, over-worn sofa and started massaging his forehead with his massive hand. He seemed transfixed by his own thoughts while rubbing his forehead. He finally looked up at Ramona.

"Baby, please sit down," his words a whisper. "I'm confused, babe."

Ramona opened her mouth to speak, and Churchill silenced her gently placing two fingers on her lips.

"Sweetie, Mona, you know I grew up around here. As a young man, I never had or even thought to get a driver's license. Everything I needed or wanted was right in the neighborhood. I could never see past Baltimore."

"Growing up in urban America, you don't experience a lot of the outside world. You're simply an innocent, ignorant victim of society's manipulation and manifestation. Like that family that died on Harlem Avenue, like the brothers in the 'Nam, we're all victims. The worst part, I felt helpless. Before, I always felt strong, but with all this death, drug dealing, and apathy, I feel lost and helpless for the first time in my life.

"Look at me, nineteen, drafted into the army, and I choose the Marines. I gits sent to Parris Island for basic training, and next, I've got a big knife and a gun trooping through Vietnam."

Churchill waved his hands in the direction of his feet.

"Mona, I'd never been out of Baltimore."

He was on a roll now and didn't even stop to catch his breath.

"My first job in Vietnam was to secure a foothold and direct helicopter assaults. I was first in and last out. Once I was on the ground, my responsibility was to call in close support, and that usually meant a Cobra attack. I'd make a call, and all of a sudden this monster helicopter is overhead or heading in fast.

"When you see an attack helicopter in action, you will never forget it. Once that monster tips its tail, it's a matter of seconds before an arsenal of rockets and twenty millimeter Vulcan cannon shells are spewing death. The damn thing comes in fast, and I'm asking for fire around me. I was ground zero. Blood, guts, and the stench of death were everywhere.

"The worst I saw was when we first locked up with bad-ass VC. That's what we called them Viet Cong. The battle lasted for over a month. No matter what anyone tells you, they were tough, fearless, and motivated. Dey been fighting the French, the Chinese, the Cambodians, and anybody who messed with their land for over ah hundred years. Now it was us.

"Anyway, what happened next was almost an accident. I drop onto a landing zone near their base camp, just as an enemy patrol is coming by, and it was on. The VC wanted a quick victory, and we countered with all our available firepower. We didn't know they had eight thousand troops at their base camp.

"After it was all said and done, over three thousand enemy troops died, and I don't know how many we lost."

Churchill shook his head as he remembered his fallen comrades.

"The American story at the end of the engagement was that untested American soldiers had defeated the best light infantry in the world. That was basically the case, but we paid a helluva price. I was never the same after that, and it never leaves me.

"Yeah, I saw some rough stuff on the streets of Baltimore, but nothing can prepare you for the 'Nam. There was always a sinister overtone at play. The natives that smiled in your face could become your deadliest enemies. It was a matter of life and death every day. We lost a lot of friends and good brothers. It was truly hell on earth.

"Almost all the brothers filled roles like mine. We were the grunts, front line, so it was get busy killing from jump street for the brothers. When I got to the 'Nam, I was nothing but a streetwise punk, and I had to learn the ropes real quick. The brothers taught me to survive. A funny thing happened when we had a chance to talk. The brothers were almost all from urban America---New York, Philly, Detroit, Chi-town, Oakland, L.A., Cleveland,

and New Orleans, just drafted and serving. We found out we came from the same situation. Our neighborhoods were the same. Our people faced the same indignities. We'd lost family and good friends to the streets and drugs, and nobody cared. We were kindred spirits. We became friends and brothers.

"When I got out, I applied for disability for this wound and didn't get one red cent. Nothin! I go to the Veterans Hospital, and they give me a couple of aspirin and tell me to take it easy. I'm pissing blood and get aspirin.

"I try to find work. Nothin! Telling somebody you a Vietnam vet don't mean shit. Actually, it works against you. There ain't no great demand for trained killers. Everywhere I see destruction of our men, women, and children to drugs and the violence that comes from the drug world. The damn dealers are getting rich and being glorified as heroes. In the meantime, people are looking at me like a fucking street derelict.

"Next, you hear about the cadavers of enlisted men being used to ship heroin and whatever into the country. Again, somebody's getting rich exporting drugs, contraband, or whatever in the bodies of my friends and brothers from the war. You talk about a twisted world. Where's the heroin going? Right fucking next door!

"I was a mental wreck behind all that. I was losing it and losing it fast. The physical was bad but that psych thing. Whewww! And, it's like there's nothing I can do. Nobody cares."

"I care," whispered Ramona.

Churchill smiled, looking deeply into her teary eyes.

"I know, babe."

He continued in a tortured whisper.

"I suffered through depression. I turned to alcohol and drugs. That's when I got lucky and hooked up with you. My eyes opened, and I realized that being a man was more than occupying a body; it came with the responsibility of your convictions and the necessity to overcome difficult situations. I realized that was the definition of a man. You made me reach into myself.

"I remembered how hard the Vietnamese fought for their country. I talked to the brothers from the war, and they made me understand how I fit into the picture America had created for us as blacks. I'm going to work with them to make a difference for you and me."

Ramona jumped into Churchill's arms, kissing him passionately and forcing him down onto the sofa.

CHAPTER FIVE

"Leaving the shelter of the nest,
I fear oblivion and contemplate soaring.
But is soaring a reflection of temporal success
and security, Or is it akin to stemming
the torrential tides of life,
Thus courting oblivion?"

Judge Abrams watched the courtroom maneuverings between the prosecutor and defendant with extreme interest. She had presided over hundreds of trials and had a sense of the unfolding drama. To her surprise, she was not discounting the defendant's chances at trial. There was something in his carriage and demeanor that impressed her. She despised Gosselin and felt he was due for a comeuppance. This may just be it. The thought resonated in her mind. *Obviously, the preponderance of evidence is against the defendant, but I've seen strange things happen in courtrooms. It's not the right or wrong. It's the law and the jury's perception of the law.*

Trey was deep in thought as the prosecution opened its argument. He deferred the opening and closing arguments to the prosecution, feigning ignorance and a lack of preparation. Gosselin accepted to demonstrate his superiority and ingratiate himself to Judge Abrams. Trey thought, *He's underestimating me. He thinks I'm completely ignorant of procedure and totally unprepared.* Smiling, he thought, *Great for me.*

His mind dashed between the events at hand and Harlem Avenue. *I don't understand why, but I seem to be reliving my past. Maybe this is not the best time.* Without realizing it, his thoughts flowed to the person who started this odyssey, the man named Connie Gordon.

☙❧☙

Growing up, James Marion "Connie" Gordon worked with his father in the District of Columbia selling fruit and vegetables to a fleet of pushcart and truck street vendors. They worked out of a small warehouse in Northeast D.C. located between New York and Rhode Island avenues. The young Gordon was industrious, directed, and ambitious until he saw the movie "Superfly."

He venerated the movie and its main character to the point of seeing it well over twenty times. He constantly talked of being like Priest, the hero and main character. He was determined to possess all the material trappings displayed in the movie. Unfortunately, those trappings were eerily consistent with those of street pimps and drug dealers.

He sold hot dogs and peanuts at RFK Stadium in the summer to get into the games and find a way to rub elbows with higher-ups and athletes. This trait tended to follow him through his adolescence and into his young adult life.

His father had hoped that he would grow out of his infatuation with material things and settle into the lifestyle of an honest businessman, but it was not to be. It seemed that young man had an almost psychotic bent to the criminal, and it manifested itself in all of his outlets, even his speech and demeanor. It became a constant source of friction and conflict between the two. The younger Gordon seemed to prefer dishonest business even when he could easily accomplish the same ends dealing honestly and aboveboard. He always schemed to get over on someone.

As a youth and young adult, Gordon frequently subjected his friends in Washington to slick moves and con games. These miscreant deeds earned Gordon the nickname "Connie." He liked the moniker, and it stuck for life. He seemed to live to find his next victim. Whether it was screwing a friend's girl, not repaying a debt, or stiffing someone in a drug transaction, he was always busy.

He was a big man with stunning good looks and was charismatic to a fault. He was a "yellow" black man with light skin, hazel eyes, and "good hair," which meant that his hair was fairly straight unlike the curly or kinky hair that most blacks had. His hair grew very fast, and often he'd get it processed into the flowing "Priest-look" of his hero from "Superfly." He also had a taste for expensive cars, flashy clothes, and jewelry. He never lost an opportunity to demonstrate his conspicuous gains.

On the surface, Connie was clean as a whistle. But to know him well was to tolerate or to hate him. He was the kind of guy who would give a party, and, long before the party was due to end, he would abruptly turn on the lights and instruct everyone to leave. His motive for "turning out the party" was to get rid of any excess guys and invite the most attractive women to a more private set.

The conflict between him and his father escalated to the point that his father gave him an ultimatum.

"Son, there are fifty states in the United States of America. I live in the District. Pick your own place to live." Cleverly, Connie enrolled at Central State College in Xenia, Ohio. In short order, however, he returned to the District by transferring to Howard University and ultimately even conned his father.

While at Howard, he was arrested in a bootleg T-shirt and liquor operation but considered the arrest the price of doing business. He was able to grease the right palms, and each charge mysteriously disappeared. When he was arrested again on a liquor sales tax violation, his father emphatically told him, "I'm not tolerating any more affronts to my reputation because you got to play slick. I will not tolerate crime being associated with the Gordon name in the District. Now, I brought you into this world, and I will take you out. You got ta go."

After this confrontation, Connie decided to move to Baltimore. He saw Baltimore as fertile territory for his con games and those "Baltimorons" as the perfect patsies for his schemes. He would still be close enough to the District to take advantage of situations there, but he'd put some distance between himself and his father. In Baltimore, he saw the opportunity for his greatest con. It wasn't the District, but it beat the proverbial blank.

Connie knew he had the looks, connections, and wealth to establish himself as a major player in Baltimore politics. His minor offenses could be swept aside, so he would appear to be a perfectly legitimate businessman. On the surface, Connie was a successful Baltimore real estate broker, bail bondsman, and partner in an insurance company. The businesses were all fronts, the laundering apparatus for the millions he was making from cocaine, marijuana, and heroin distribution. He had been refused a patronage appointment to the city's liquor board after an in-depth check on his background found him linked with gambling and unsavory associates.

However, using the tricks he had mastered in D.C., he quickly made the right connections in Baltimore. He threw lavish parties and invited stunningly beautiful women from Washington to introduce to his newfound friends in Baltimore. He made sure that the women met the powers-that-be in the city, and he nurtured their clandestine relationships. Most of the men were married, so he found himself in their confidence. They shared jokes of their conquests, and he egged them into more decadent pursuits. He made sure that he supported their charities, campaigns, and lifestyles with money and gifts.

After twelve years, Connie was on important Rolodexes all over Baltimore. Now he was ready for bigger and better things. Coincidentally, a member of the Maryland Democratic Central Committee called Connie.

"Hey Connie, guess what? Marla Washington just died, leaving a vacancy in the General Assembly. Know anybody interested in the seat?"

Smiling from ear to ear, Connie replied, "Yes, I think I know the perfect candidate."

Connie swung into action, reserving half of the forty-five rooms at The Tides Hotel on Miami's South Beach, a classic hotel in taste and design, with each of its large rooms decorated in muted shades of cream and white and looking directly over the beach. It was the perfect choice for Connie's plans, offering luxury, premium service, sensuality, and elegance.

He invited key members from the nominating committee, his lady friends from D.C., and the power brokers in Baltimore.

"I'm throwing a big party for my friends in Miami," he bragged, "and you really don't want to miss this one. You pay your transportation, and I've got the rest. Be there."

They readily accepted his invitation, and Connie smilingly rubbed his hands at his good fortune. Everything went as planned, and Connie was at his best as he lobbied and was promised endorsements for the vacant seat. *Just goes to show you what a little money in the right places can do for you*, mused Connie.

While in Miami, Connie slept with the wife of Morris Campbell, one of the men who had helped him on the committee and when he first arrived in Baltimore. Over the years, he had slept with several such women. He formed no attachments from these sexual adventures and used the conquests to further his business and political ambitions. It privately amused him that he was cuckolding the "Baltimorons," and the women were giving him ammunition to screw their husbands big time.

Linda Campbell fell madly for Connie and showered him with gifts, sex, and attention. Unknown to Connie, Linda's husband Morris had already begun to distrust him. There were rumors about major drug connections, graft, and kickbacks. Even worse were the tales of Connie calling his benefactors "Baltimorons" and sleeping with their wives behind their backs.

When Morris Campbell first heard the rumors, he encouraged the gossiping to stop.

"For the good of us all and the political agenda at hand" would be his politically correct statement. Then he heard the rumor about Connie and his wife. He put this together with his wife's change in attitude, varying schedule, and declaration of love for another man. That man could only be Connie.

Morris pressed his wife about her infidelity, and she sneered.

"You want to know. Okay then, Connie and I are lovers, and I'm gonna be with him. You haven't been there for me; it's always business and politics."

He shook with anger and fury. The pain of the revelations reverberated through his soul. It stung his heart deeply to think about losing his wife and hurting his children.

"Yeah, and Connie told me about you and those bitches from D.C.," Linda continued. "Yeah, you been a playboy while I'm home with the kids. Yeah nigger, I'm the dumb bunny. Let's see who gets the last laugh in this. Connie and I started in Miami while you were playing power broker, and we've been meeting at the Brown's Motel ever since."

The words had barely escaped her lips when Campbell swung a swift open-handed blow to the left side of her face. Linda stumbled backward and tumbled to the floor.

Morris clenched and unclenched his fists, sucking air through his teeth. He reached for Linda.

"Damn! Damn! I'm sorry, I'm sorry. Shit!"

Linda's face shifted from shock to fear to hatred. She slowly got up and straightened her dress. She looked with laser eyes as her lips twisted into a snarl causing her to taste the blood in her mouth. Speechless, she left the room.

Morris's fury swung to Connie, and he angrily vowed, "I'll get that son-of-a-bitch if it's the last thing I do!"

He calmed himself and ran after his wife thinking, *I can't let Connie know that I'm onto him.*

"If you want Connie, I'll bow out, but we've got to keep things cool and out of the public eye for the sake of the children," he pleaded. His plea seemed to assuage Linda, and she waved her hand and turned her back dismissing him.

Morris began to make discreet inquiries into Connie's real estate, insurance, and bail bond holdings. It quickly became clear that Connie was dealing from the bottom of the deck. He was infuriated even more by Connie's solicitous behavior toward him, and he did his best not to let Connie know he was now dealing with an enemy. Morris recalled the old saying, *Revenge is a dish best served cold.*

He discovered that Connie was receiving large quantities of drugs from New York to be parceled out to smaller dealers in Baltimore and Washington. Morris realized that Connie was making tremendous money and virtually never getting his hands dirty.

It's funny, he thought, what a little money could buy. Revenge is at hand, and it's going to be sweet and simple. It's time to drop a dime on

Connie.

Morris recorded a muffled message detailing Connie's drug activities and connections. He found three different pay telephones and played the anonymous message to the Baltimore City Police Department, the state police, and the Federal Bureau of Investigation.

Within two months, the FBI had arrested Connie outside the Maryland State House in Annapolis as he was leaving a night legislative session of the General Assembly. He was charged with conspiring to transport millions of dollars worth of raw heroin from New York City to Baltimore over a two-year period of time. His arrest sent reverberations up and down the Eastern seaboard.

ತಿಜಾತ

"That stupid, egotistical, son-of-a-bitch!" thundered Darius Jenkins from his posh home in Staten Island, New York. "I set up this bitch with a gravy-ass situation in Baltimore and what does he do? He becomes a fucking politician! Who the fuck does he think he is, Adam Clayton Powell or somethin'? Gonna be the first nigga in the Oval Office? That stupid son-of-a-bitch is compromising us all. I knew that nigga's ego was going to get us in trouble. I knew it! I knew it!" Darius screamed.

Jack "Jackie" Jackson had never seen him this angry before and nervously looked at the door behind him.

"Ya see, Jackie, I been telling Connie about how he got to be invisible. All he had to do was move the shit in Baltimore and to D.C. What's he do? Becomes a fucking delegate in the fucking Maryland General Assembly. Ain't that a bitch? He probably fucked over somebody in Baltimore, and they dropped a dime on his dumb ass. Color him a memory. Color this motherfucker a memory! I'm going to ventilate his fucking brain!"

Darius "WeeWee" Jenkins had moved from Durham, North Carolina to the Big Apple fifteen years earlier. He had become a major narcotics trafficker, moving the product directly to New York and redistributing it in Philadelphia, Baltimore, and the District. His idea of reversing the flow of drugs from the traditional south-north runs had made him a millionaire many times over.

He was the country boy who made it big in the big city. He was a quiet-living man and was the only black in the Staten Island neighborhood where he resided with his three children and twenty-three-year-old girlfriend. He appeared to be a legitimate businessman with holdings in the North Carolina Furniture Company in Queens and Jenkins Enterprises and Jenkins Realty Company in Brooklyn. He owned a Rolls-Royce, a Jaguar, and a Mercedes-Benz two-seater sports car.

Now he had a problem big enough to put him out of business, land him in jail, or even get him killed. Jenkins knew that the problem was one Connie Gordon, and it had to be eliminated one way or another.

CHAPTER SIX

*"Taking the less-traveled road,
portends pain, loss and obstinate circumstances."*

Trey looked lovingly at his father in the courtroom, but his heart sank at the signs of age and worry on his face. His mother smiled, and he saw her clutch the Right Reverend's arm and pull him close. Trey returned the smile and nodded, trying to send a message of assurance and hope. *Sometimes the son must become the father.* The thought brought a new intensity and focus to his demeanor.

As the prosecution ended its opening argument, Trey's mind turned to his father and memories of the Right Reverend in the pulpit preaching. It seemed like a million years since he sat in the front pew of little Cornerstone Baptist Church and watched his father deliver fire and brimstone to save the souls of his congregation. He saw the Right Reverend standing like a monument behind the pulpit. Pride resonated in his soul, knowing he was the offspring of this proud and forceful man.

The Right Reverend John Ballard had nurtured tiny Cornerstone from a storefront church into one of Baltimore's largest congregations. In doing so, he had also become one of the most politically powerful ministers in the city. His congregation had grown so large that two Sunday services were needed, and the pastor contemplated adding a third.

Still, there was more to Reverend Ballard's ministry than pastoring, weddings, and funerals. Cornerstone was a platform for the Civil Rights Movement. He'd worked with Dr. King and gained notoriety, political power, and the local establishment's contempt.

Trey would never forget the passion in his father's eyes and face as he screamed his verbal attacks on the society with regard to the plight of the Negro in America. The sermons always ended with his father's clear, methodical, and even-toned pleas to his congregation on the need for Negroes to achieve their civil rights.

The Right Reverend was a huge man with a huge Afro and a thundering voice. He had worked in the cotton fields of Mississippi and as a stevedore in Baltimore before finding his calling in the church and with civil rights. Although he was a man of the cloth, he was not a man to be taken lightly in a physical sense. When the Right Reverend became angry or agitated, his son need only look at his father's massive hands and know that the law was being laid down, and he had better follow it.

The towering pastor grew up in the largely rural, relatively poor, cotton-growing Mississippi Delta area. Mississippi was the standard bearer for the South's resistance to racial equality, leading the nation in what are now called hate crimes. It would have been the first state to secede from the Union, before the Civil War, if South Carolina had not done so first.

Ghosts of Mississippi haunted the Right Reverend. No place in America could evoke the emotions of this flat and lush land. Mississippi was a deadly paradox. It was a heat-blistered paradise that covered its Nazi-like regime with a mint-julep facade. It was the deadliest place in America if you were a Negro.

The Mississippi State Sovereignty Commission, the Mississippi Citizen's Council, and the Ku Klux Klan were the tools of the Negro's repression in the state, and they had the sympathy and cooperation of local law enforcement. In its heyday, this triumvirate's mission was to wage war on the freedom movement, to keep the Negro down, and to monitor the activities of everyone or anyone wishing to alter the status quo of the Mississippi way of life. To them, the Right Reverend was one of those subversives who would Africanize the country and the glorious state of Mississippi.

The Right Reverend would never be able to purge completely this past from his memory. It permanently altered his view of his destiny in the larger world. He became convinced that Negroes would have to make their own destiny without white assistance. He became increasingly radical and knew he had to get out of the

Delta as soon as reasonably possible. Mississippi was the Right Reverend's training ground and would make him what he was to become.

Trey remembered the look on the Right Reverend's face when he blasted Spiro Theodore Agnew.

"That son-of-a-she-devil," the Right Reverend, rarely using profanity, yelled. "The Vice President of the United States and from Maryland is discussing authorizing segregated schools. I might as well be back in Mississippi for this," he bellowed. That Sunday, the congregation would get its fill of Agnew and Maryland politics.

"Why, we may as well go back to Mississippi or the islands as slaves," he thundered from the pulpit.

"The Vietnam casualty list is growing, as are reports of veterans' addictions," the Right Reverend vented.

Trey began to hear about drugs more and more every day. He heard it on the streets, at the dinner table, and would hear it in church on Sunday. Not a day went by without some discourse from someone. By now, the Right Reverend was fed up with the heroin situation and was determined to get his message across. He was a teetotaler and abhorred drug and alcohol abuse in any form. He planned a sermon that would set the parishioners' ears on fire and attack the addiction demons.

Collections for the construction of a newer and larger Cornerstone Baptist Church had begun, and the Right Reverend was becoming a fixture on the news commenting on this issue or that situation.

The following Sunday, the Right Reverend wore his black robe with African designs on the lapels. From his seat behind the pulpit, he rose and slowly approached it. He surveyed the congregation slowly until you could hear a pin drop. The only audible sound was the voice of a restless child. The minister started to speak in a consistent monotone with his head bowed.

"All praise be to God. Can I get an amen?" The congregation replied in a fairly subdued tone, "Amen."

The Right Reverend started the monotone again, but his pitch began to rise.

"I will begin this Sunday's sermon on a poison that is flowing through the blood of our society. My main question is, why do people choose to use drugs to destroy their lives and the lives of everyone they come into contact with?" He allowed the words to hang in the air.

"Heroin users will steal from their mothers, fathers, sisters, and brothers to feed their habits. They will use their rent money, take food from the mouths of their children, and even sell their bodies to feed this filthy, disgusting habit." His face was drenched in contempt as he shook his head.

"The Mayo Clinic in Minnesota, you know, one of the most prestigious hospitals and research facilities in this country, has reported that it may be possible to cure drug addiction with a brain operation." He laughed while shaking his head sarcastically.

"Did anyone ask the Mayo Clinic who was going to pay for all these brain operations? God and morality are the only operation needed for these people. Can I get an amen?"

"Amen!" thundered the congregation.

"Stanford University, another one of these prestigious institutions, has been conducting experiments on monkeys to find out more about heroin users. Monkeys!" He bellowed before bowing and shaking his head in a mocking manner.

"I'm glad they chose monkeys this time instead of the Negro men down at Tuskegee. And I'm definitely staying clear of that old Negro monkey comparison."

Laughter spilled from the congregation.

"Anyway, Stanford University, this prestigious institution, reports that the only prerequisite for heroin addiction may be the availability of the drug and a willingness to try it."

The minister's eyes blazed as he paused for effect.

"If these people were available to God and willing to listen to His word, they wouldn't need to be shooting this poison in their arms! Can I get an amen?"

"Amen!" the congregation roared, really getting into the sermon now.

"Let me go on," the Right Reverend's voice trailed off as he lifted his hands to stem the tide of emotion growing within the congregation.

"A New York City College professor, a man of education, has testified before Congress that the greatest sources of hard drugs in large cities are policemen and narcotics agents. Can you believe that?

"Let's look at it this way," he continued while wiping his thick brow. "The very people paid and empowered to stop this destruction. The very people!"

The congregation's excitement grew with each word.

"The policemen and the federal agents are selling what they seize in drug raids. Their desire for money has completely overridden their moral and sworn duty to keep this poison off the streets. They have actually become instruments of death themselves."

The Right Reverend's voice grew with intensity.

"A drug war has been raging all over this country. Gary, Indiana has reported its seventeenth death associated with the cocaine and heroin wars. Detroit, Michigan has reported fifty deaths associated with the so-called drug wars. It's bad enough they're killing each other, but now they're killing innocent women and children. They are killing everybody for their love of money and drugs!" he shouted with contempt as he picked up the pace of his oratory.

"A report from the Surgeon General has indicated that heroin addiction is on the increase and spreading from large metropolitan centers to smaller cities and towns. The report says that the number of heroin addicts has increased from 300,000 earlier this year to as many as 800,000 now. That means the number of addicts has almost tripled in less than a year. We are talking about approximately one million people in this country addicted to heroin. Now, that's a lot of brain operations!"

His attempt at humor drew a spatter of laughter from the congregation.

"In Chicago, a group identified by police as the De Mau Maus are saying no to drugs in their community. These young men have declared war on drug dealers. According to the police, our protectors, the De Mau Maus, have also declared war on them. The New York professor just informed us that the greatest sources of hard drugs in large cities are policemen and narcotics agents. Who's guilty here?"

The Right Reverend gave the congregation an incredulous look.

The church fell silent, and then there was nothing but his thunderous roar.

"Black soldiers in Vietnam have set up unofficial drug counseling programs to help addicted black enlisted men. They're saying that heroin or skag or whatever you want to call this poison is a problem threatening to derail the Black Power movement.

"In Harlem, in New York City, black youths have declared a war on Harlem pushers. They've created liberated zones to be free of dope and dope dealers. They say that they are not going to be polite about this, and they're going to start in the street with the pusher and work up! They want the higher-ups!"

The pastor calmed down again.

"I say them Harlem black youths are smart. I say them Harlem black youths are onto something because I don't see no poppy fields growing around here."

"I don't see nobody around here getting super rich or superfly from drug dealing. All I see is strung-out, destitute, and dying people. I say the problem is at the top. I don't see no arms factories around here, but people are getting shot every day. When Martin had his dream, it surely was not this. Any mountaintop I have ever seen had a clear and fresh view. Not genocide, not the view from this mountaintop."

The congregation was stirred and hung on every word.

Starting slowly again, he emphasized each word. "Martin and Malcolm died to give us an opportunity for freedom."

He paused. "Somehow that freedom has translated from mountaintops and African vistas to guns and shipments of drugs. Dope and bullets. Drugs and money. Death and no future. We are not being shipped jobs, education, or food. We are being shipped alcohol, cigarettes, drugs, guns, and death!" The reverend's voice literally shook the rafters, and the reverberations from the amplifiers echoed through the neighborhood.

"Those black Harlem youths are right. We here in Baltimore need to search our collective consciousness and find a way to combat this menace. This is just plain old good versus evil. I'm not suggesting vigilantism, and I believe Gordon Parks said it best. We have a choice of weapons. Teach the children the best we can. Set a daily example for how they should live. Build the next bigger and more powerful Cornerstone Baptist Church. Keep a smile on your face when you want to cry. Make wrongs right, or just live every day as Christians."

The Right Reverend sure could talk, thought Trey, and he made sense.

Reverend Ballard's voice and politics had long before traveled beyond little Cornerstone Baptist. From voter registration to police brutality, the Right Reverend was a voice for the people of the city. Trey was so proud to be his son. He and his father did not vocalize their love, but it was there.

As Trey left the church, he saw Churchill. He ran to his surrogate big brother and smiled.

"Churchill, how ya doing?"

"Solid, little Trey. How you?"

Churchill returned his smile and engaged him in a hand dap.

"Your father was on a roll today. You could hear him all the way up and down Harlem Avenue, and darn if he wasn't making sense. I know he don't like me much, but you always remember I'll be there for you both. I gotta go, little soldier, but take care, and I'll see ya later."

"Yeah later," replied Trey after Churchill had already left, but "later" had come to mean "whenever."

It seemed that Churchill was always going somewhere lately. Even when he wasn't, his mind was elsewhere. Still, it was comforting to see him even if just for a time.

CHAPTER SEVEN

"Whilst expedience may forestall the great
consequences in life, And afford the traveler
immediate self-gratification,
It perchance condemns the
follower to a rudderless path."

Trey's opening argument left Judge Abrams fighting to mask her favorable impression of him. She thought, *His opening was well conceived and presented.* Trey exhaled slowly as he returned to his chair accompanied by a smattering of applause, which was quickly silenced by the judge's gavel.

Trey fought to stop his knees from shaking and found the tremors were threatening to extend through his entire body. He dropped his head, pretending to sort through the papers in front of him. He was pleased with his opening, but his heart pounded as if it were about to come through his chest. He composed himself as he replayed his opening in his mind. After a few minutes, an agonizing thought slammed into his brain, *This is still all about that son-of-a-bitch Gordon.*

ଓଔଔ

As soon as Connie made bail and was released from jail, he retreated to his posh digs in downtown Baltimore. He knew he had to talk to WeeWee as soon as possible but couldn't risk using his telephone. WeeWee had warned him long ago to maintain a low profile, but he insisted that he knew better. Now he had to face WeeWee's wrath.

Connie peered from behind drawn curtains in his Park Place apartment. He lived on the fourteenth floor of the fifteen-story complex in exclusive Bolton Hill. From his high vantage point, he saw reporters and casual observers on the sidewalk below. They had been camped outside most of the day. He stalked the apartment like a caged tiger, finally slamming his fist hard onto the kitchen table.

He switched on the television and radio but eventually heard "James Marion Gordon" and "drug bust" lumped in the same sentence. Pacing, he found himself constantly peering outside. As dusk settled, he saw the reporters packing to leave. With nightfall, the street was empty.

Connie waited until after 2 a.m. and slipped out of his apartment. He padded slowly through the lobby and tiptoed past the sleeping security guard to the elevator that would take him to the basement garage.

He slid into his black Cadillac Eldorado and breathed a sigh of relief as the powerful engine roared to life. His head darted from side to side to see if he'd aroused anyone's attention. When he didn't see anyone, he breathed a deeper sigh and gained solace as the Cadillac's soft, leather seats enfolded him. Darkness enshrouded his vehicle as it slipped out of the garage onto Park Avenue. He breathed another sigh of relief when he didn't see any reporters. *It's funny*, he thought. *At this moment, I have a greater fear of the press than the police.*

The urban Baltimore settings transformed into suburbia as he entered Baltimore County. He glanced at Brown's Motel on Route 40 West, remembering his many liaisons there. For some reason, Linda Campbell struck a chord, but he shook his head thinking, *The last thing I need now is some butt.* He drove until he reached the countryside of Columbia and made a left, losing his own way on the dark, back-country roads. *At least I know I wasn't followed*, he thought. He found a gas station in a little out-of-the-way place called Wilde Lake and stopped in front of the pay telephone.

"Wee, it's me," he said tremulously into the receiver.

"Where are you?" the responder was clearly perturbed.

"I'm on a pay telephone in the sticks," Connie replied trying to be as ingratiating as possible. The response was succinct and cold.

"Give me the number, and wait 'til I call back." Connie gave him the number and hung up to a click. He didn't know what he was going to say to WeeWee, but he knew not talking was a death sentence. So here he was.

It seemed that minutes ago he was sitting in the General Assembly, plotting his rise to the governorship. He could see it so clearly. He'd play the same games he'd played on those dumb-ass Baltimorons, only at a higher level. He had already finagled his appointment to the House of Delegates.

Boy, I worked that crew. The timely death of Delegate Washington, calling in my markers, and some not too subtle pressure on the committee had swung me the recommendation. Not only that but some bedroom talk had contributed to my selection. He smiled thinking of the men he'd cuckolded and the women who had been his pawns.

I forced my way in, and that would be the first of many shrewd moves to come. I'll be a power broker supreme, and part of my reward will be screwing the Caucasian wives of my delegate cronies.

Connie loved the idea of working in Annapolis. From its earliest days, the Annapolis State House was known as the "Athens of America." The State House has an excellent view of Annapolis harbor. The beautiful blue water of the Chesapeake Bay glistened in the distance as small sailboats bobbed at their moorings or floated lazily on the choppy waters.

Annapolis was the capital of Maryland even though Baltimore was the largest city in the state. Connie had seen a significant number of blacks in the area and thought, *This is fertile ground to build on.*

Immediately after his appointment, Connie drove around Annapolis looking at the neighborhoods, houses, and gathering spots. He wanted to ensure he had the right address and associates. He couldn't help but admire the many types and styles of homes characteristic of the town that was also home to the Naval Academy.

In the past, a thriving shipping industry had brought great wealth to Annapolis. Prosperous merchants and planters sought to duplicate the amenities of their British homeland in the colonies and built mansions that would rival any in England. Many of the Founding Fathers had been entertained in these formal ballrooms and gardens. Annapolis had more of the original 18th-century structures standing than any other city in the United States.

Government always played a major part in the ongoing operations of Annapolis. The Annapolis State House was where George Washington tendered his resignation as General of the Continental Army, hastening the end of the Revolutionary War. A smile had crossed Connie's face when he thought about it. This will be the world of James Marion Gordon. Governor Gordon had a nice ring to it, fits right in there with Jefferson, Madison, and Washington.

Connie startled at the ring of the pay telephone. He awoke to the realization that he was in the middle of nowhere and trying to stay alive. He cautiously picked up the receiver.

"Wee?"

"Yeah Connie. You sure this is a clean connection?" a stern voice blurted out.

"Yeah Wee, definitely. I'm on a pay telephone in the middle of nowhere, and I couldn't have been followed."

The solicitous tone seemed strange coming from Connie's tongue, but survival instincts had taken hold, and, like a chameleon, he had changed his colors.

"Well Connie, I really don't know what to tell you," WeeWee stated flatly while thinking, *All the times I've tried to advise this motherfucker to maintain a low profile, and it didn't do a damn bit of good.*

"Do you know what evidence they have against you?"

"Not everything Wee, but I understand they got an informant and maybe some wiretaps."

"Am I implicated?"

"I, I don't know, Wee, but I'd sure tell you if I did."

"Look Connie. I'm going to send a couple of the boys down to nose around and see what they can pick up. Call me in a couple of days while we let somma this dust settle. When you call, make sure you're not followed, and change the pay telephone location. You got it?"

"Yeah Wee, we're going to get out of this, and I'll never implicate you no matter what happens."

"All right, Connie, let's see what happens. Call in a couple of days, and don't be followed."

"OK Wee, I'll get back to you and keep you outta this."

The telephone went dead in his hands.

"Life's a bitch!" Connie screamed into the night.

WeeWee turned to the two men standing behind him at the pay telephone. Staring hard at his associates, WeeWee spoke deliberately. His North Carolina accent emerged with his anger.

"This is real simple, brothers. Go down there. See how messy this thing is. If he can't get out of this without implicating us, off him, and make him a memory." He continued his icy stare while waiting for acknowledgment.

Nervously, Jackie, the larger and more menacing of the duo, replied, "No problem Wee, I never liked the motherfucker anyway."

Twenty days later, Connie left his apartment and slipped into the garage well after midnight. He had agreed to call every two days following the same basic pattern. Life had been a roller coaster ride for Connie. The first days after his indictment were pure hell, and recriminations flew everywhere.

Connie immediately went into action, refusing to cooperate with the prosecutor. Grandstanding in front of the press, he proclaimed both his innocence and confidence that he'd prevail at trial. He chose a highly influential attorney who adeptly filed to move his trial to a federal district court in another jurisdiction.

The prosecution openly expressed concern about the case: "Gordon has gone to the mat and is fighting the charges." Connie's highly publicized arrest sparked charges and countercharges between the Democratic and Republican members of the General Assembly. It all reminded Connie of the set-up for many of his schemes and one of his favorite sayings. "If you can't blind them with brilliance, baffle them with bullshit."

Connie began to feel good about the situation and believed he could make a favorable report to WeeWee. For the first time, he looked forward to his late night drive into the countryside. He theorized, *I might be able to weasel my way out, and most importantly, without implicating WeeWee. My political career is over, but Wee and I can go on making millions.*

He was lost in thought as he pulled the keys to his Cadillac out of his pocket. He excitedly tossed the car keys in the air, thinking of just what to say to WeeWee, but he fumbled to catch them. He found himself smiling. *I'll let WeeWee know that I'm working my way out of the situation, and my allies are going to the mat for me. Yeah, I'm going to get out of this thing. I'll start playing the Democrats against the Republicans and even start shoveling some of their shit around.*

The first genuine smile since his arrest creased his face.

Jackie and Carlton "Cutty" Cutler, WeeWee's two lieutenants, lurked in the shadows of the garage. They looked at each other and shook their heads as Connie fumbled with his keys. Jackie remembered, *Yeah, this is the motherfucker who tried to play on my woman in New York. She told me how he'd come across talking about me.*

WeeWee wouldn't let him retaliate at the time because of business, but he knew that people like Connie always found a way to mess up. He had prayed that one day he would be the person to settle the score. Now, Jackie fingered his double-barreled, sawed-off shotgun and kissed its bluish-black steel barrel. He relished the idea of putting out Connie's lights. He couldn't kill him badly enough.

Jackie's movement forward was halted as he saw three figures moving in the dark to his left. He jerked his head back and a barely audible "Whoa!" escaped his lips. He tapped Cutty and pointed in the direction of the silent figures before slipping further into the shadows. They took a safe vantage point from which to observe Connie and the three figures dressed in camouflage and wearing ski masks. Ducking behind cars, the three moved quickly toward Connie.

Jackie and Cutty eyed each other, silently signaling their admiration for the stealth and deadly approach they were witnessing. Jackie pointed to Connie and rolled his eyes, signaling that he was an idiot. Jackie couldn't help thinking, This place is getting as crowded as Grand Central Station, and this idiot is oblivious to it all.

Moving like cats, the three camouflaged figures continued their approach until Connie was surrounded with his hands high in the air. He shook violently, and his eyes bulged with fear, which made him look like a stereotyped character played by Mantan Moreland. Jackie fully expected to see Connie pee the pants of his beige, double-knit suit.

"You are a known drug dealer, selling drugs in the black community. You are a despoiler of our women. These are acts of treason, and the penalty for treason is death," Connie's antagonists yelled. As Connie opened his mouth, the massive leader punched him hard in the face screaming, "Shut the fuck up, you yellow-livered, drug-dealing pig!"

Connie whimpered and sniveled like a baby, and the leader turned to his henchmen.

"And he's a punk motherfucker too." He slapped Connie. "Stop crying, bitch."

"Please, please don't kill me," Connie pleaded, rubbing his hands together, begging hysterically.

Shaking his head, the muscular leader cut into Connie with six shots from a .38-caliber revolver.

The shots ripped into Connie's torso, splattering blood and guts against the side of his Cadillac. He continued his dance with death by gripping at his wounds as if he could pull out the damaging projectiles. Connie slumped against his car and slowly slid to the ground. As he looked up at his assailants and attempted to speak, another man leaned over and with a knife slashed deeply into Connie's throat.

"I'll bleed you like the pig you are, punk!"

A third assailant slowly stepped to Connie and pumped a shotgun blast into his already lead-filled chest. As the echo from the shotgun blast died, smoke and the acrid smell of cordite filled the air. The garage was suddenly silent as a tomb. The leader disdainfully tossed multi-colored leaflets over and beside the body. The three figures disappeared as quickly as they had appeared.

Wow! is all Jackie could think.

WeeWee always said don't mess with them Baltimoreans, and I think he's right.

He turned to Cutty and whispered, "Let's get outta here, but be careful. We have to duck those guys and anyone else who may have heard."

The next day, Jackie stood before WeeWee listening. "It looks like you and Cutty were a little overzealous, huh? No matter. I knew when I assigned you to our little problem that you didn't like him, but wasn't this a little bit of overkill?" Smiling, WeeWee put a giant snifter of Remy Martin to his lips.

Pausing for effect, Jackie smiled. "We didn't do a thing, boss."

WeeWee's head snapped around, spilling the cognac down his front and onto his favorite leather chair.

CHAPTER EIGHT

"Biased, rugged terrain constricts
the path to true love,
And beckons loss into a slippery, black hole."

Anxiety gripped Trey as the trial moved to its evidentiary stage. *This will be the most dangerous part of the trial for me. I have no trial experience, and I have to know when to object. Gosselin's confident and has the power of his office at his disposal. Focus, man, focus. Put your mind to work.*

Trey's mind drifted to being old enough to go downtown alone and watch trials at the various Baltimore courts. He fancied himself as an attorney working for the defense. He noticed a predominance of black people on trial and a judicial system dominated by whites. The judges, attorneys, clerk, bailiff, and security were all typically white. Basically no different than now, the system's continuing racism brought a sardonic smile to his creased face.

To his young, fertile mind, the Baltimore judicial system seemed a big part of the economy. Huge courthouses dominated the middle section of the city, and the black masses were under a constant barrage of criminal, civil, and traffic offenses. He thought of the trials he'd witnessed and the times he wanted to scream at defendants not to self-incriminate. He had seen serious criminal trials, but he enjoyed civil and traffic court most because the trials were often very humorous.

A smile crossed his face when he thought of the traffic trial of an 80-year-old white woman. She had been charged with running a red light, smashing through a fence, and coming to a rest after crashing into a statue. The judge asked the woman for her driver's license, and after fishing around in her purse for the better part of a minute, she handed a document to the judge.

The judge looked at the document and dropped his head trying to suppress laughter. The entire courtroom sat on the edge of its seats anxiously awaiting the judge's response.

Controlling his laughter, he said, "Madam, do you realize that this is a 1941 California learner's permit?"

The entire courtroom burst into laughter. The woman had been driving for decades without proper credentials.

Trey thought, *No black person in Baltimore could hope to get away with that for thirty days.*

The smile from his reminiscence quickly disappeared as his thoughts jumped to finding a way to prove his innocence.

That reporter in Baltimore tried to prove my innocence. Jerry something was his name. He may yet be able to help me.

ଔଊଔ

The telephone's shrill ring awakened Gerald "Jerry" Freider. Rolling over, he rubbed his eyes and looked at his alarm clock that displayed 2:44 a.m. His thoughts screamed, *Who could possibly be calling me at this hour?* He fumbled for his glasses while simultaneously knocking the receiver off the hook. He stuck his glasses crookedly on his face and retrieved the fallen telephone receiver.

"Who is this?"

"This is a member of Black October. Delegate James Marion Gordon, better known as Connie Gordon, has just been executed," the baritone voice shot through the receiver.

Sitting up in his bed, Jerry fumbled for the pen and pad on the nightstand by his bed. He thanked himself for the discipline to have them available. The original purpose was to record ideas conjured up in his dreams. He thought abstractly, *When you do the right thing, good things happen for you.*

"Who is this again?" he shouted into the receiver, settling into an upright position.

Very slowly and deliberately, the baritone spoke.

"This is a member of Black October. Delegate James Marion Gordon, better known as Connie Gordon, has just been executed."

"You mean the Delegate Gordon, the one under the drug indictment, is dead?"

"Yes," the baritone barked.

"How do you know?"

The deep voice continued in a monotone.

"Black October did it. Gordon has paid the price for pushing drugs in the black community."

Incredulous and confused, Freider tried to gain his composure and shift to a reporter's stance.

"How? Uh, was he shot?" was the best he could get out.

"Yes. He was shot in the chest with a shotgun, six times with a .38 caliber revolver, and his pig throat was cut."

Jerry was busy jotting everything on his pad.

"Where's the body?" He felt inept in response and pressed his brain for a higher level of focus and cognizance.

"He was executed in the basement garage of the Park Place Apartments."

"Is that all?" Jerry asked still confused. He wanted to slap himself for not verbally engaging the caller and drawing out more information.

"What, ya want him deader than that?"

The caller hung up.

Jerry's brow wrinkled, and he rubbed his hand hard across his forehead and down his face. He rubbed his eyes as he pondered the call. He quickly decided to err on the side of caution and called the police.

Jerry had been a reporter at *The Sun* for twelve years. He had gotten a by-line, but it was in the local "Marylander" section of the newspaper. Rarely did he have a story with what he considered real meat. In his opinion, he was on the dog show, human-interest circuit. He never had an article appear on the front page and had begun to question whether he would find real success in the newspaper business.

He willed his mind to focus on the telephone call with the realization that he might have his first blockbuster by-line. Even though the news was heinous, he reminded himself the only bad news is no news. Jerry recounted the telephone call and left his telephone number with the police. He rushed to the shower.

The Sun was located between Calvert Street and Guilford Avenue just northeast of downtown. The area conveyed an industrial park look because it was adjacent to a viaduct and a dead-end street. Jerry thought about the locations and offices of The *Washington Post* and other major papers for which he longed to work. Originally from New York City, Jerry had hoped he'd be back home or working in another major market by now. He felt stuck in the drudgery of local reporting in Baltimore. Complicating the scenario, he had been at odds with his editor and had come close to quitting.

The telephone rang as Jerry emerged from the shower.

"Hello," he answered on the second ring.

"Mr. Freider, this is Sergeant Dempsey calling on behalf of Commander Bauer."

"Yes sergeant."

"Mr. Freider, the commander wants you to know that the information you reported was essentially correct, and you need to be available to the police for questioning as soon as possible."

"No problem, sergeant, just let me know when and where you need me."

A greedy smile crossed Jerry's face as he pulled clothes onto his wet body.

Henry H. Bauer, commander of the Baltimore City Police Department's Homicide Unit, dressed and rushed to the crime scene.

Bauer's responsibilites were to provide highly complex staff assistance to the department's chief. His work required considerable judgment in the interpretation and application of rules, regulations, laws, and ordinances. Considerable latitude was permitted for independent action within the framework of department and division policies. He generally reported to and received direction from the chief.

By the time he arrived at the police station, information was flooding in. First, the call from Freider, and then a call from security at Park Place, all saying the same thing. Connie Gordon was dead.

The initial murder report struck an ominous cord of déjà vu as Romy Mason's murder crossed Bauer's mind. He had seen a number of murders over the years that fit this modus operandi. Since they were minor black drug dealers and not under his protection, they were quickly swept into the unsolved murder files.

His initial speculation was that Gordon had been hit by his drug connection from New York City. But the Black October call to Freider put another spin on things. He knew Black October had been discounted as a political splinter group looking for some form of recognition. He contemplated the situation as he held the three different color leaflets strewn near Gordon's bullet-ridden body. Bauer had seen similar pamphlets that read:

This person is a known drug dealer. Selling drugs is an act of treason. The penalty for treason is death.
Black October

He rubbed his chin as his focus shifted to the actual commission of the crime.

"Uuumm," he mumbled while deep in thought. *There are only two ways to enter Gordon's apartment complex. Either you pass the building guard in the lobby, or insert an access card to open the garage door from the outside. The building has a closed circuit security system, and it was operating, but reports indicated the pictures from the garage were very fuzzy. The pictures on the other security cameras were crystal clear.*

Commander Bauer talked to the detectives to ensure he would receive all incoming information as soon as possible. There were no reports of shots fired, and the building guard told him:

"I didn't see or hear a thing"

Connie was killed two stories below the lobby, and Bauer found the location to be a lonely and isolated place. So the guard's story was plausible, and he chose not to press him further. Probably asleep anyway, Bauer imagined.

Detectives found several tenants who said they heard gunshots during the night, but they all added, "This is Baltimore. We hear gunshots all the time."

Bauer could see that the slaying was well planned and speculated that the perpetrators slipped into the garage behind an incoming automobile, maybe even Gordon's. Gordon had his wallet and credit cards but no money. Bauer did not believe that robbery was the motive.

The next day, Bauer stood before the press.

"The anonymous caller's information to Gerald Freider of *The Sun* was so correct, and the call came so soon after the murder, that it must have come from a person with direct knowledge of the slaying. However, we tend to discount the involvement of this clandestine group calling itself Black October.

"Aside from crudely painted slogans on a number of buildings in East and West Baltimore, little is known about the group or whether it exists in any tangible form. This murder has the earmarking of a gangland or professional contract slaying. Links have been established between Mr. Gordon and a reputed millionaire drug czar in New York. The garage's closed-circuit television was put out of commission. We will work all angles on this case, and we will find the killer or killers."

Commander Bauer finished by saying, "There will be no questions at this time. That is all." He immediately spun to his left and marched away from the microphones and buzz of the press.

Bauer believed WeeWee Jenkins had ordered Gordon's slaying because he feared implication. He knew Jenkins was smart enough to cover his tracks by shifting the blame onto a low visibility and possibly non-violent group to cover his tracks. He didn't think that Black October, if there were a Black October, had the expertise to pull off such a professional and complicated slaying. Plus, he'd never seen blacks organize anything effectively in Baltimore, even a killing.

A report of a taxicab hijacking the night of Gordon's slaying was really throwing him for a loop. Strangely, an almost identical incident had taken place a month earlier. Jenkins certainly would not have been inclined to start plotting Gordon's death at that point. Each incident involved two men flagging down a cab in Northwest Baltimore and asking to go to a nearby intersection. If the taxicab hijacking were related to Gordon's slaying, then there was a group operating in Baltimore. If that were the case, then it was time for Bauer and Baltimore's finest to knock heads with Black October.

CHAPTER NINE

"Yet, in survival, the lessons in faith, love and devotion,

**Magnify and glorify the relationship,
Thus creating an unassailable bond."**

Trey listened in the classic Malcolm X pose as Gosselin presented the evidence against him. Gosselin was adept at pulling damning statements out of witnesses. He started his examination with the warden from Lorton. As Gosselin questioned the warden, Trey remembered the day in 1972 when he was taken to the Baltimore City Jail and relieved of all personal possessions. He most hated seeing his Baltimore Polytechnic Institute graduation ring tossed aside with a lack of deference.

He was forced to strip and then was sprayed up and down with a water and powder solution to prevent or kill lice. Finally, a white powder was dashed against the front and back of his body as he held up his scrotum. As he walked out of the crudely designed shower stall, he was handed an orange jumpsuit and a pair of Styrofoam slippers. The jumpsuit was two sizes too big, forcing him to roll up the sleeves and pant legs.

Trey looked up to see a black man staring at him from behind the kind of bars reserved for vicious animals at the zoo. The man was over six foot, three inches tall with massive, perfectly sculpted muscles. Even though he was behind the extra thick bars, he had wrist and leg restraints. The look of the man was not one of intimidation, though he stared in an unblinking manner. Trey wondered, *What is he in here for? Why is he so greatly restrained?* The penetrating look from his eyes told a tale of woe. Trey now knew that feeling.

Jerry Freider's first headline graced the front page of *The Sun:*
Indicted State Delegate Slain

Jerry knew he was on to something. He had that gut feeling that reporters were supposed to get about a story.

Black October was real, and it had knocked off that scumbag Gordon. Its political agenda was obviously the eradication of narcotics in the black community. This could be Pulitzer Prize stuff.

He slowly rubbed his hands together in delight.

He went to see Adell Amos Hilton, the Baltimore State's Attorney, who, earlier in the year, had said that he had received calls from people saying they were speaking for Black October.

Hilton said to Jerry, "We really don't know much about Black October. They appear to be without a face and without a body. They are a mystery, but everybody in the black community knows they're real."

Freider tried to reach Gordon's lawyer, but his secretary said that he was in Europe on an extended vacation. Jerry excitedly thought, *This is getting better by the second. His instincts now told him the police were off the mark pursuing the gangland aspect of the slaying. The chilling call I got the night of the slaying leaves no doubt in my mind that Black October is the culprit. Plus, the police don't have any explanations for the leaflets. I've never heard of a gangland slaying that used such a ruse to throw off the police. This was political and pointed to the existence of a group impassioned enough to kill and to publicize its agenda. And it appears that I'll have an open playing field to pursue the Black October angle.*

He thought with glee, *Black October, Pulitzer Prize, and Gerald Freider.* Only now there was a problem. He didn't know where to go from here. Black October was a mystery,"...With no face or body."

His euphoria dissipated as he realized, *It isn't as if I could go gallivanting through East and West Baltimore's inner city on an undercover mission. This isn't "Black Like Me." The only thing I'd get from trying something that stupid would be six feet of dirt and the right to push up daisies. Shit.* He cast his eyes down and thought about a stiff shot of Jack Daniels. He was stuck.

A month passed, and the ringing of his telephone again awakened Jerry. Noting the hour of the call, 12:27 a.m., Jerry silently prayed it was Black October. This time he was more focused and allowed the telephone to ring while he picked up his pad and pen and settled into a writing position.

"Hello. Who is this?" Jerry said into the receiver.

"This is a member of Black October. Freddie Brown has just been killed."

This time the voice was muffled and distorted. Jerry pumped his fists into the air and raised his head to the sky thanking God for the break. He sat back and tried to relax.

"Who is this? And how do you know?"

He thought, *You've got to find a way to work this much better than last time.*

The distorted voice began again.

"Jerry, we are willing to use you as our media pipeline. So far you've been fair to us. We will feed you the first details of our activities as long as you cooperate, and don't ask stupid questions. Now, I am a member of Black October, and I know Freddie Brown was executed because Black October did it. Freddie Brown has paid the price for pushing drugs just like Connie Gordon."

"Was he shot like Gordon?" Jerry shot back.

"No, Freddie Brown was," the muffled voice made sure to emphasize the word was, "only shot five times with a .38-caliber revolver."

"Who is Freddie Brown?"

"He was a known drug pusher and a traitor to the black community. He was the next to be eliminated, and he will not be the last as long as drugs are a scourge to our community."

"Where is the body?" Jerry asked quickly.

"It's on the lawn on Allison Way in the Pimlico area of Northwest Baltimore."

"Is that all?" inquired Jerry, not believing his good luck and quickly jotting down the words of the speaker.

"No. You will receive a written statement from Black October on our position. The statement will explain that Black October will even go to the extent of execution to stop drug trafficking in the black community. We found it hard to kill a member of our black family, but we hope to be able to scare brothers and sisters out of the dope business."

Jerry fell back onto his bed dumbfounded. He quickly called the police department and insisted on speaking to Commander Bauer. He was put on hold for what seemed like an eternity, and finally someone stated flatly, "The Commander will call you right back."

Ten minutes later, Commander Bauer called in an exasperated tone.

"Mr. Freider, I understand that you've gotten another message from Black October."

Jerry rapidly spilled words recounting the conversation.

"Oh Commander," Jerry added, "the caller also said I was going to get a written statement on Black October's position. I don't know how they plan to deliver it, but I thought you should know." The commander thanked him and hung up.

Commander Bauer was at home in a foul mood when he spoke to Jerry. He had again been awakened in the middle of the night with news of a slaying. Worse still, these slayings were making headline news, not like the typical murders of blacks in Baltimore. He was on the carpet, and it wasn't good.

Bauer was a disciplined man due to his West Point training and years in the military. After retiring at the rank of colonel, he assumed civil law enforcement would be less taxing and dangerous than the military. In Baltimore, he had found a new war zone and one with no clear objective or enemy. For years, he'd suffered through constant, irrational violence with no end in sight. He'd wanted to make a difference but came to believe that policing Baltimore City was like trying to plug twenty leaks in a dam with ten fingers. That's when he started thinking, *Fuck this. I'm going to get paid any fuckin' way I can. Now this Black October shit could derail everything.*

"Damn!" he heard himself exclaim as he kicked the covers off his bed. Bauer knew that shit flowed downhill, and his exasperation was going to be pressed onto someone else.

"Fuck it all!" he exclaimed as he swung his legs out of bed.

☙❧☙

Jerry threw on his clothes and raced out of his house. He wasn't particularly concerned about going to the crime scene, knowing police officers had been dispatched, and he wasn't going into the bowels of West or East Baltimore. The northwest Baltimore neighborhood near the famed Pimlico racetrack was considered a fairly safe community. However, in recent years, the Reisterstown Road and Park Heights Avenue corridors had gained a reputation for its young killers. To Jerry's understanding, this stemmed from its transformation from an upper-middle-class Jewish community into a middle-class black community. The black kids in the neighborhood found themselves under constant assault from toughs from East and West Baltimore. They were outnumbered, and their assailants were experienced and vicious. Their disturbing and rapidly increasing response was gunplay, and it had become one of the customs of the community. A stray thought hit Jerry's mind as he rushed to the location. *This will definitely be a murder scene, which means Black October is for real.*

Jerry was immediately relieved to see the red, blue, and white lights of the marked and unmarked police cars illuminating the night. He saw a covered figure lying on the lawn with Commander Bauer standing prominently nearby. He was obviously in a very ugly mood and started kicking at weeds and pacing in a small circle.

Yellow crime tape cordoned off the area, and Jerry was even more relieved when he noticed he was the only reporter present. A young police officer challenged him as he approached the police tape, but Commander Bauer waved him through. Jerry walked directly to the commander and immediately saw leaflets with the familiar signature "Black October, Off the Pusher" message. Another group of leaflets contained the following:

This person is a known dope dealer.
He has made his living
off black people for a long time.
He has paid the penalty for treason.

There is no hope in dope.
Save our black children.

Jerry stooped to pick up one of each type leaflet, raising alarms from the detectives, but again Commander Bauer waved them off. Jerry wanted to thank Bauer, but he saw the anger on his face as he watched his men go about their work.

Jerry rushed to his office to start writing his article. As he pulled out his notes and the leaflets, he noticed a strange envelope on his desk. Jerry snatched the envelope and anxiously tore it open. It contained a typewritten statement from Black October.

Jerry pursed his lips and nodded his head in grudging approval as he realized that whoever was doing this was very much ahead of him and the police. He ran to make copies of the statement and then called the commander. He smiled to himself when his call was immediately sent to Bauer.

Jerry's next article in the paper covered the murder of Freddie Brown and its possible link to the Connie Gordon murder. He told of his late night call from Black October and the copies of leaflets found at Brown's murder scene. Lastly, he included the printed statement found on his desk:

Brother Jerry.

This is a statement from the men and women of Black October. We want it to be known that we were brought into existence firstly because of the ever increasing problem of drugs, drug addiction, and related problems. We know that it is known that drugs account for better than 90% of the crime in the black community.

It is also the cause of the chaos and confusion and distrust present amongst our people. Not only this, it threatens our very existence by destroying our young and taking away their desire to live, build, and create. It turns our hope of the future into a threat of the present.

This is why we feel that it is necessary now, after many years of depending on corrupt police, to solve our own problems by any means necessary and available. As you have witnessed at this point it is hard to tell who sells more dope, the police, or the pushers. It seems that every ounce that is confiscated, sooner or later finds its way back onto the street.

It is common sense that the only one that will ever sincerely do any-

thing for black people is black people. And even God or Allah helps those that help themselves.

We found it hard to kill a member of our family (black people). But one who would sell poison to our children we no longer consider a part of our family. So was the case with [Delegate James Marion] Connie Gordon. We hope to scare brothers and sisters out of the dope business but we are ready to go to the extent of execution if necessary, as you have seen.

The machine gun on the leaflet is the symbol of one firing group in Black October, the one that executed Connie Gordon. Our organizational sign is the scales representing popular justice, the people's justice. We will always try to leave leaflets explaining our moves whenever possible.

We also have sent letters to black community leaders asking them for support.

Dope must go
Save black children
Off the pushers
BLACK OCTOBER

The next day, Commander Bauer stared straight ahead at his press conference.

"Again, the anonymous caller's information to Gerald Freider of the *The Sun* was so correct, and the call came so soon after Freddie Brown's murder, that it must have come from a person with direct knowledge of the slaying. We no longer discount the involvement of the group known as Black October. To date, no links have been established between the Gordon and Brown deaths. That is all for now."

Again, the commander spun on his heels with characteristic military precision and stalked away.

Bauer now believed Black October was involved in Gordon's murder.

Jenkins and his mob would not go to this extent to cover up Gordon's murder. Plus, the FBI and New York City Police Department were covering Jenkins closely. Obviously, there was a Black October with the expertise to pull off professional and complicated slayings. It also had the foresight to deliver the statement to the press before I had a chance to intercept it or even know it was coming. They're making me look bad. My police force has been accused of drug dealing, and I had to recant an earlier statement.

"I'm going to get these motherfuckers if it's the last thing I do, and now I've got clues to work with," he said aloud to no one in particular.

I'll investigate the taxicab thing and the statement from Black October referencing firing groups. That's a military term and one used in Vietnam. Maybe I'm dealing with Vietnam veterans here. I'll check the production of the leaflets and the reference to Allah. Maybe the Black Muslims in the city are involved.

He involuntarily looked at his balled fists, realizing that his knuckles were white. *Jerry Freider is the only direct link to Black October, and I'll keep a close eye on him. Wiretaps have already been authorized on his home and office, and an officer has been assigned to keep constant surveillance on him. The break for the case may come through Freider, in effect making him my wild card. That's why I'm giving that prissy Jewish son-of-a-bitch leeway I wouldn't otherwise consider.* Another thought invaded his mind. *It's time for Baltimore's finest to put the Lorenzo Stomp on Black October, and I don't want it to be pretty.*

The Black October story was making Jerry's career. He wasn't reporting to the dog circuit editor anymore and was getting extreme deference from his colleagues. Most important of all, his by-line was on the front page of every edition. He loved his newfound adoration and the hefty bonus that accompanied each by-line.

But there was something else; he actually respected whoever was doing this. He did not believe in killing but respected the sentiment that had kindled it. Drugs had been a real problem in the black community for many years, and it took real guts to make this kind of stand. Maybe there was something he could do to prevent a recurrence of the Black Panthers' shootouts with police in Chicago and Oakland. He sensed the same type of violence coming to the streets of Baltimore and felt the hairs on his arms rise with alarm.

Jerry focused on the case, studying the autopsy and crime scene reports. He had fashioned himself into an investigative reporter with a real story on his hands. He found that Freddie Brown had been acquitted of the only narcotics charge brought against him but was convicted of a violation of the Deadly Weapons Act and had received an eighteen-month sentence.

Brown indeed had five .38 caliber bullets removed from his body, and there was evidence to support that he was shot with more than one gun. He had bullets in his upper chest, lower back, right thigh, and flank. Jerry smiled, thinking, *Someone on the Black October firing team is undisciplined or a comedian because Brown was shot in the ass. Hey, I just said firing team. Is that my instinct supporting the contention that someone with military experience was involved? If so, five will get you ten that it has to be Vietnam vets.*

"Hmmm," he found himself saying.

Jerry went to the funeral for Freddie Brown and later saw expensive Cadillacs and Lincolns parked in front of his home. He tried to interview family members but had to retreat, encountering strong resistance and even a threat to "break your fucking neck." He realized these people had money and were not to be trifled with at all.

He developed sources on the streets to monitor known narcotics distribution areas. His sources reported a growing sense of caution among dealers but no discernible slowdown in the rate of traffic.

This is far from over. This could take on a life much greater than the murders of Connie Gordon and Freddie Brown, he surmised.

⋘⋙

"WeeWee" Jenkins was now off the Baltimore police radar. He'd planned to knock off Connie and had sent the men to do it, but they didn't do it. Nevertheless, the FBI and New York City police continued probing his finances, his businesses and his associations. At one point, the authorities had actually come to his home on Staten Island and roughed him up.

WeeWee's empire was unraveling in front of him.

"If that damn Connie wasn't dead, I'd kill him myself!" he screamed. WeeWee knew he would be at risk if he were arrested, and now the weight Connie felt was suddenly on him. There were people in New Jersey and New York who would silence him because he knew too much.

WeeWee felt he had two choices, make a deal or run. He chose to run.

He was in Las Vegas when he was arrested and extradited back to New York on charges of tax evasion. His bail was set at $5 million, his passport was revoked, and his travel restricted to within one hundred miles of New York City.

WeeWee made bail and immediately skipped again. This time he was arrested in North Carolina and again extradited back to New York. In response to his second arrest, authorities confiscated his home and cars and froze all of his assets. He was further charged with attempting to sell 100 pounds of heroin and cocaine at a street value of $38 million.

After WeeWee's arrest and the death of Connie Gordon, a rumor circulated that WeeWee was an underling of the Black Mafia out of Harlem, having ties to the Italian Mafia that peddled heroin and cocaine.

☙❧☙

Carlo "Lolo" Rosiello's face was red with anger as he fumed over the newspaper reports.

He started screaming, "Those nigger bastards don't even know when they got something good going. They don't respect a goddamn thing!"

The Mafia captain thrust his face close to the man in front of him and spittle sprayed from his lips as he continued to rant.

You, "call that nigger Lonny and tell him that he better clean this shit up, and we better not hear another goddamned thing about it."

The telephone rang at Lonny Logan's swank Harlem apartment. Anger and frustration registered on Lonny's face as he bit his lip trying to respond favorably to the venom spilling from the other end of the telephone. Anger poured from every pore of his body.

"Yes, I understand. No, it won't be a problem. Yes, I know the importance of our relationship. No, I wouldn't want to jeopardize our families or the business. OK. Yes. No. All right, I'm sure you'll be satisfied."

He hung up the telephone slowly while exhaling through clenched teeth. And then, he flung the telephone across the room.

"Motherfucker! Talking to me like that," he yelled.

Andre Adams was Lonny's right-hand man. He was not used to seeing Lonny placate anyone or even lose composure to the level he had witnessed. They had been through what seemed like a thousand wars and even though Lonny hadn't done any wet work in years, he knew he was more than capable.

As Lonny looked up, Andre quickly said, "I know he's got to go." Lonny's scowl seemed to grow exponentially as he nodded his head up and down.

The day WeeWee was released into the general population, he thought, *My connections finally got me out of isolation*.

Suddenly, a huge shadow fell on him from behind. As he spun to face it, he caught the glint of the prison shank as it tore into his stomach and then up into his heart.

The giant figure wielding the knife pulled WeeWee close enough to whisper, "This is a present from Lonny. Goodbye Wee."

WeeWee's meteoric career as a drug czar was over, and Connie was still screwing people from the grave.

ଔଔଔ

"Mr. Freider," Commander Bauer barked into the receiver, "since you have been so helpful and supportive to us in this Black October investigation, I thought you'd like to go cover our first Black October arrest."

"Great Commander Bauer, when, where, and how?" Jerry responded with delight.

"Be at the precinct at 10:30 tonight, and don't be late."

"Thanks a million, sir. See you there." Jerry excitedly hung up the telephone, thinking about his next by-line.

Bauer turned to his lieutenant and said, "I can't wait to hear what that sanctimonious motherfucker has to say about this."

CHAPTER TEN

"Pain and trepidation are intrinsic to the thorny path,
And, absence requisite,
Perhaps, leaving the child shoeless, wanton, and lonely."

Trey squirmed in his seat as Gosselin continued calling witnesses. It seemed a never-ending parade of indictments against him. The jury cut contemptuous looks in Trey's direction, and Gosselin seemed completely in control. A sourness rose from Trey's stomach as Gosselin built his case.

Trey's mind drifted to the night he lounged in the basement of his parents' home. He watched television as the sounds of Isaac Hayes' "Hot Buttered Soul" played in the background. He loved nothing better than listening to this album and "The Isaac Hayes Movement" during his good-night telephone conversations with his main lady, Candace. His parents constantly questioned how he could concentrate with so many things going on at the same time.

By now, Trey had moved from the upstairs bedroom he shared with Clifton, so he could fashion a sanctuary in the basement of the house. He had a television, stereo, and waterbed. The walls were decorated with black light posters of scantily clad women and his sports heroes and music idols. His parents hated the room, but they tolerated the situation, knowing that he would soon be back at Howard University.

ଔଔଔ

One night late in the evening, Trey heard a loud banging on the front door. He looked at the clock and saw that it was 11:30. *Who the heck could this be?*

"Candace, somebody's at the front door. I better get it before Dad goes crazy. I'll see you tomorrow, and remember I love you."

He blew a kiss into the receiver.

"I love you too," came her reply.

Trey dashed up the steps to beat his father to the door, wanting to be the first one to confront the annoyance. He assumed it was one of his crazy friends.

But whoever it was should know better than to knock on the Right Reverend's door at this hour. The thought puzzled him.

He remembered his mother waking him early one morning last year saying he had a visitor. She was a great practical joker, which was belied by her stern demeanor.

As Trey stepped through the front door, he saw a white BMW idling in the street and a friend lying prone on the lawn. Apparently, the guy had passed out from liquor, drugs, or a combination thereof. Why he had come to his house, Trey didn't know. He recalled sheepishly looking at his parents and shrugging as he carried his friend into the house. He could only hope this was not another such episode.

As he approached the door, the Right Reverend was midway down the corridor heading for it as well. Trey gave him a pained expression, trying to say he was sorry, and it's probably somebody he knew. The Right Reverend gave him a look of disgust, pivoted, and retreated up to his bedroom. He heard murmurs coming from his parents' room as he peered through the peephole.

He jerked back in surprise upon seeing two city police officers standing on the stoop. He immediately thought, *This has something to do with my car.* From his meager savings, Trey had purchased a beautiful, robin's egg blue, 1970 Mercury Cougar with a white vinyl top. It had an immaculate white interior, white wall tires, and chrome steel wire rims that perfectly accentuated the car's colors and profile.

The car was not only a showpiece but also a muscle car with a limited edition Cleveland 351-cubic-inch motor. It was one of the fastest assembly cars ever built. He and his buddies constantly raced their cars.

Police always stopped him at the beginning and end of each month. Trey understood he represented a security blanket and a safe stop every month. He surmised that the police had a quota of cars to check fitting his car's profile. They knew he was not one of the young Baltimore killers they could stumble across if they truly made random stops. After initially being upset, he realized it worked to his advantage.

But now Trey didn't recognize either of the cops and called up to his father in a strained voice.

"Dad, it's the police."

The Right Reverend was at his side in an instant, pushing past Trey and peering through the peephole. He turned to look at Trey as he opened the door. The look on the Right Reverend's face asked, *What have you done now?*

Deeply concerned now, Trey shrugged his shoulders. The Right Reverend opened the door.

"Officers, what can I do for you?"

A large, burly officer fingered his service revolver as a smaller officer stepped forward saying, "We're looking for a Mr. John Ballard the third."

"That's me," Trey responded.

"Mr. Ballard, you're under arrest." The smaller officer stepped past the Right Reverend to seize Trey. He roughly turned him around and applied handcuffs while looking the Right Reverend directly in the eyes. The burly officer moved in front of Trey with his hand on his revolver.

"This is my son. What's this about?" shouted the Right Reverend.

"Sir," replied the smaller officer, "your son is under arrest for murder, kidnapping, assault, and robbery. We have a search and seizure warrant for this address, and we expect your full cooperation."

ଓଓଓ

The next day, the headline in *The Sun* screamed:
Suspect Charged In Gordon Slaying
Radio station WJZK led its morning news with "A 20-year-old Northwest Baltimore man was charged yesterday with the murder of Delegate James Marion Gordon. Gordon had been awaiting trial on federal narcotics charges when he was found shot

to death in the basement garage of his Park Place apartment tower."

Jerry had the front page and his by-line again. But something just didn't seem right to him.

The suspect was twenty years old, a college student living with his father, a prominent Baptist minister and civil rights leader. Of course, that didn't mean the son was like the father. But the look of fear and bewilderment on the young man's face as he was led away sent chills up my spine.

The search of the house uncovered a .38-caliber revolver and several rifles licensed to the minister. This wouldn't be unusual because the minister was an avid hunter. There was a double-barreled shotgun, Winchester lever-action rifle, Remington 30.06, and the .38, which reportedly was hidden. Other evidence was said to have been seized that Jerry didn't see coming out of the house.

The police supposedly had been led to the younger Ballard because his fingerprint had been found on a Black October flyer at the scene of Gordon's murder. Moreover, a heel print at the murder scene matched a shoe confiscated from Ballard's home. Jerry wrote his by-line story, but he had a gnawing feeling that something was rotten in the state of Maryland.

Trey was arraigned on homicide, kidnapping, robbery, assault, and possession of a dangerous weapon charges. The court held him without bail and scheduled a preliminary hearing in two weeks.

Jerry called the Right Reverend and asked if he could visit the home. He explained his doubts about Trey's involvement and that he wanted to tell the family's sides in his articles. Begrudgingly, the Right Reverend consented. Soon after his arrival, Jerry watched as the family and friends bowed heads and clasped hands in a circle. The Right Reverend led them in prayer.

Jerry could see that Trey's family, friends, and neighbors were in shock. The environment was as quiet and solemn as a tomb. Trey's sister, Brenda, had returned home from college and took up residence in his room. She paced somberly through the house with tears visible in her eyes. Trey's brother Clifton was catatonic, sitting and staring with the assembled entourage in the family home.

After seeing the family's reactions and support, Jerry was convinced the police had the wrong man. He interviewed the neighbors who were effusive, their hands flying in all directions.

"He's always been a contributing member of this community, a direct support to my children, courteous to everyone on the block and, on top of that, he's a serious and outstanding student. We all know and respect the family. Trey's a great person, someone you would want for your friend." There were no negative comments.

Back in his office, Jerry stalked from the window to his desk. He looked at the half-written article, knowing it had to be on the editor's desk within the hour. His brow was knitted, and his lips pursed. He felt disconnected from everything other than Black October and Trey Ballard. The Trey situation simply made no sense to him. He briefly smiled when he realized that he was doing substantive reporting, but it quickly disappeared.

He wanted to be fair in his reporting, but the editors were hammering him for sensationalism and adherence to the company line of writing stories that would sell the paper and disparage the innocent. Sadly, the company line did not support his gut feeling about Trey's role. He jumped behind his typewriter and pecked out the article, walking the razor blade between editorial license and the company line. When he was satisfied that the material would pass muster, he snatched the paper out of the typewriter and yelled for the copy boy.

"Jimmy, take this to the copy desk." He was surprised at his authoritative tone and quickly apologized.

"I'm sorry, Jimmy, but this Black October stuff is getting to me. Please take this to Barry. He's waiting on it. Thanks. I'm leaving for the day."

He made his way home with something gnawing at him. Jerry popped open a Budweiser as he clicked on the television, paying no attention as the screen came to life. Instead, he retreated to the kitchen and pulled out a glass tumbler and tossed in three ice cubes. He felt the comfort of the square bottle of Jack Daniel's and let it caress his palm. He held the bottle in the air and looked at it, enjoying the amber color of the liquid and slowly started pouring the amber liquid over the ice. He poured until it was near the rim and shook his head at the indulgence. He picked up the tumbler and the Budweiser and went to his favorite chair.

Jerry sipped his Budweiser and gulped Jack Daniel's, drinking himself into a stupor.

This story has changed my life forever. The by-lines are great, and the money even better, but are they worth my dignity and soul?

Jerry was awakened from his drunken stupor by the ringing of his telephone. He stumbled to his bedroom, shaking his head and rolling his tongue over the ugly aftertaste in his mouth.

"Hello!"

"Brother Jerry, this is a member of Black October." The voice was a different one but still muffled and distorted.

"The police have arrested the wrong man, and we are going to prove it. You will receive another statement indicating that Mr. Ballard could not be and has never been a member of Black October. Black October is responsible for the executions of Delegate James Marion Gordon and Freddie Brown."

The line went dead.

This time Jerry was so drunk, and the call ended so quickly, that he never picked up his pad and pen. As his mind cleared, the actual message registered, snapping him into cognizance. He staggered three steps backward and reached for a chair to keep from falling. The caller had said Trey Ballard wasn't guilty, and Black October was going to prove it. He quickly thought, *I've got to get Bauer to replay the message for me. Naw, fuck it. I'll ad-lib it.*

The next day, Jerry sat at his desk nursing an Alka Seltzer and water. Jimmy walked in and tossed a stack of mail in front of him, causing Jerry to recoil in pain.

"Rough night, huh?" Jimmy asked. "It looks like you really tied one on."

"Shoot me," Jerry shot back.

"Hang in there, Mr. Freider. Don't let this stuff get to you. Oh, by the way, this envelope looks like the other one you got from Black October."

Jerry's head snapped up, and his eyes cleared. When he grabbed the envelope, Jerry immediately knew it was from Black October. He shook his head.

"These guys are good." Jerry's mind was rolling.

They've outfoxed Bauer again. He briefly toyed with the idea of giving the envelope to Bauer's people to preserve as much forensics as possible, but the thought process sent pain through his alcohol-soaked brain.

"Fuck Bauer. I'm a journalist," he said ripping open the envelope.

The envelope contained another typewritten statement from Black October. He jumped up from his desk to race to the copier, but a pain shot from his spine directly to his brain, and he collapsed back into his seat with a mumble.

"I'll never drink again," knowing it was a lie. As he approached the copier, a police officer walked in and took the document from his hand. He gave Jerry a disdainful look as he placed the document in an evidence bag.

Jerry protested, "Hey, what are you doing?"

With a smug look the officer said flatly, "Officially, the Baltimore City Police Department is seizing this as evidence. If you have a problem, take it up with your editor."

Jerry dropped his head on his desk saying, "Shit, shit, I'm fucking up!" He stumbled out of his seat thinking, *This is the first time I'm actually interested in seeing my editor.*

Barry Simpson, Jerry's editor, looked at him with questioning eyes.

"Jerry, I gave orders that all Black October materials go directly to the police. The deal included a promise of exclusivity for our cooperation. You don't seem to be in step with the latest developments, and I suggest you get your act together. We'll get a copy of the letter before the next edition. Need I remind you that this is still a murder investigation? Get yourself together."

Jerry limped from the office stinging from Barry's wrist slap and the pain in his hungover brain.

The letter from Black October was printed in its entirety in the next edition.

Greetings Brother Jerry,

After reading and listening to the news reports surrounding the arrest of John Ballard III, we have decided to expose this attempt by the po-

lice to make him a scapegoat for our actions. First, let us make very clear the fact that John Ballard III never has, is not, and never could be a member of BLACK OCTOBER. We are not, and never will be in the habit of recruiting people like him.

We only recruit men who are motivated by that undying love for BLACK PEOPLE. At this point we are not sure just what he's motivated by. We consider the attempts to connect him to us an insult. First of all, no member of BLACK OCTOBER would be as foolish as the police have led us to believe he is.

No member of BLACK OCTOBER would execute a TRAITOR and keep all the evidence in his home, the pistol, handcuffs, blank paper, typewriter, etc. As for the typewriter, I am using it to type this letter right now.

We also used it to type up the literature found with Mr. Gordon and Mr. Brown. Secondly, the .38 [caliber] pistol is still in our possession, a fact we shall prove at a later date when we use it to execute another DRUG DEALER next month.

We would prove it this month, but all executions scheduled have been postponed so as not to give credit to the lie printed in The News American that there were five scheduled for this month. There may be ONE if we find out who said it.

We the men and women of BLACK OCTOBER sincerely hope that you, our BEAUTIFUL and INTELLIGENT BLACK BROTHERS and SISTERS, are not taken in by the lies being spread by the police.

[Signed]
WITH OUR FUTURE LIES OUR YOUTH
BLACK OCTOBER

Jerry thought about Black October's statement that Trey Ballard "…has not and never could be a member of Black October." This reinforces my opinion that Trey can't be guilty. The first slogans from Black October started to appear over ten years ago. He would have been only nine or ten at the time. The guns seized from the Ballard household belonged to the father who's a hunter, which is natural, based on his Southern, rural upbringing. Reports from the family indicated that Trey had never gone hunting with his father because he abhorred the idea of killing helpless animals. If he couldn't kill a deer, rabbit, or squirrel, would he be pumping six slugs into the body of a man? Plus, Black October claimed to have the murder weapon now.

The taxicab driver did not identify Trey, but he was still charged with the crime of kidnapping. Why would the police target Trey if he weren't guilty? Was Commander Bauer so determined to nab someone that he was using Trey as a scapegoat? The thoughts ran through Jerry's mind as he rubbed his head and neck. *Could this be retribution against the father for his politics?*

Jerry tried to think of someone in or with access to the household who could have committed the crimes. He was going nowhere fast with this line of thinking, and it only worked to send pain through his brain. *I need to get sober and stay sober because this thing is heating up.* And the the realization came to him: *Only one thing could save Trey, and that was Black October.*

CHAPTER ELEVEN

**"Yet, the prickly lessons temper the child,
Preparing him for the great challenges in life."**

Gosselin cast a ghoulish look in Trey's direction as he finished examining his witnesses. He walked to his chair smiling like a conquering hero. Trey's attempts to discredit Gosselin's witnesses were feeble if not laughable. The jury's body language clearly indicated the case was going in favor of the prosecution. Judge Abrams slumped behind the bench, seemingly dejected and disinterested.

Into this nightmare, Trey choked on the remembrance of his separation from Candace.

He was in the Baltimore City Jail with no possibility of bail. He was being interrogated regularly. He saw the good guy-bad guy routine, heard a constant barrage of questions, and suffered the hot lights and threats and deals lasting late into the night or starting early in the morning. He was isolated from the general prison population, but an inmate had already slipped by saying, "Yeah boy, you better take yoga and learn to sleep with your foot up your ass." He was in trouble. His heart was breaking and his faith crumbling.

Candace! Trey couldn't quite tell if he spoke her name or if it screamed in his brain. The idea of not seeing her, holding her and loving her was like a gash starting in his heart and moving out with the force of a nuclear explosion. *Damn, Candace, damn I'm sorry!* The words tumbled in his mind. Trey wanted anything to take his mind from the pain of incarceration. It now seemed like a lifetime had passed since he met the woman he loved.

Moving to Woodlawn, he now lived in a detached home with an expansive lawn. It was like day and night from Harlem Avenue. The Right Reverend's rural background and love of gardening had transformed the Ballards' lawn and garden into one of the most beautiful in the community. Beautiful flowers and shrubs surrounded the house, and the back yard had grapevines, apple trees, pear trees, and the Right Reverend's prized vegetable garden with tomatoes, squash, peppers, and lima beans. He even experimented with watermelons and peanuts.

The first person in Woodlawn that Trey befriended was Joseph Meade. Joe immediately invited Trey to a neighborhood party that was tremendous fun. The music was great, everyone danced, people were nice, and there was plenty of food and drink. Suddenly, Trey saw the most beautiful girl he'd ever seen sitting in the corner with two other girls.

Trey raced to Joe. "Who's that girl?"

Joe smirked and replied, "That's Candace."

Trey quickly asked, "Does she have a boyfriend? Can I meet her?"

"She's all yours, my friend, if you've got the nerve and can deal with her," Joe laughed as he walked away.

"I've had worse assignments," Trey shouted after him.

Summoning the nerve, Trey walked up to the group of girls and introduced himself. They looked at him as if he had three heads and broke out in laughter. With his tail between his legs, Trey retreated to Joe. With a sly smile on his face, Joe said, "I told you so."

Trey was never one to give up easily, and he had a strange yet strong feeling when he thought of this beautiful girl. *How can I get to know her better?*

Trey pressed Joe for everything about Candace. Joe tried to discourage his advances by saying, "Come on Trey, I know some really hip chicks that we can have a lot of fun with." Trey would hear none of it. He wanted to meet this girl and would not be swayed.

Joe informed him that she went to Milford Mill High School, and she was studious and quiet. Since Joe went to Milford, Trey was able to convince him to set up a circumstance where he could meet Candace again. Joe was cunning and, before long, he came up with a workable plan. "Trey, you're my boy. Against my better judgment, I'm going to set you up. Just make sure you're at the next dance at Milford."

At the dance, Joe led Trey to Candace and said comically and directly, "Look, this guy has been bugging me about meeting you. Why don't you give him some play?" Joe laughed, turned and walked away.

Trey looked into the beautiful brown pools of Candace's eyes and said, "I wanted to meet you from the first time I saw you. I apologize if I'm being silly, but I really find myself super attracted to you." Candace cast down her eyes.

With her eyes gazing down, Trey took in a long look at her face and body and momentarily shook and almost staggered backwards. Regaining his composure, he said, "Anyway, my name is John, but I'm called Trey. As Joe said, I know your name is Candace, but I would like to formally introduce myself," sticking out his hand.

"Hello," she said smiling and taking his hand, "nice meeting you." She looked up at Trey, and it was as if his heart stopped. An eternity passed in his mind until she said, "My name is Candace Boyer since we're doing formal introductions." Trey's reaction to her would be the same whenever they were together. He seemed at the top of the world, and his breath was gone.

Candace was a classic beauty, only five-foot-two and slender of build. She had round, firm breasts and slightly bowed legs. Her bronze skin and almond-shaped eyes flowed under long brownish black hair. Trey was in love for the first time. Trey and Candace left the dance, walked into the warm summer night, and talked while the hours slipped away like minutes. They finally settled on the bleachers of the football field holding each other and kissing for the first time.

Candace and Trey became inseparable. Candace's family immediately accepted Trey and welcomed him as an addition to the household. Trey spent so much time at the Boyers' home that his mother would call and simply ask, "Would you please send my son home?"

Candace and Trey did all the things that young lovers do. They studied together, went to the movies, parties, and dances. It seemed that they had always been close, and their special bond had always been there. What made it even better, the feelings were mutual. Everyone who knew them assumed they would marry and have children.

At another party in the neighborhood, the passion between Trey and Candace reached a level they couldn't fathom. The excitement and fun of the party left them with a desire for each other that was maddening. The nights of holding and kissing had extended to groping and questions of intercourse. Trey couldn't contain himself anymore saying, "Candace, I must have you." She shyly nodded yes.

Candace decided she would stay home from school by pretending to be sick. Trey came over soon after her mother and father left for work. They met at the door and kissed deeply. Hand-in-hand, they walked to Candace's bedroom.

Candace's bedroom was decorated like that of any young woman moving between childhood and adulthood. Trey had been in her room countless times, but this time seemed so different. There were bright colors and childhood dolls intermingled with books, cosmetics, and perfumes. Her bedroom set was white and the covers were pink. Trey's picture was on the nightstand, but today his presence in the room was awkward. Trey had been coached on what to do, but trepidation from lack of experience still played on his mind. He knew that Candace had to be doubly uncomfortable.

To make Candace feel more at ease, Trey asked if he could take off her clothes. She nodded slightly. He slowly undid her nightgown and let it fall to the floor. She stood in front of him in her bra and panties. He slowly pulled her panties to her ankles and she stepped out of them. He asked her to turn around, and he fumbled with her bra until she laughingly and mercifully said, "Let me do that."

She now turned to him, and he absorbed the bronze tone of her smooth, unblemished skin, the lush curves of her slim, ripe body, and the pert breasts that curved to the nipples he had kissed so often. He looked into her dark brown eyes and said, "I really love you Candace. I need to have your love." He felt funny because he was almost ready to cry. He looked down at the dark hairy mound between her legs and pulled her to him, resting his head on her stomach. He passed his hand down her back until it slid over her plump ass, and he felt himself grasping it firmly. Trey drank in the sight and feel of her.

Being entwined with the woman he loved clouded Trey's first sensation of sex. It was a sensation he would choose never to compromise again. She had made love to him long before he had ever touched her, and now he was floating into a state of euphoria with her.

God, his brain screamed, *there's nothing better than this in the world. He could never get enough of this woman. He wanted her now, he wanted her tomorrow, and he wanted her forever. So this was the feeling for which men so longed.*

Their eyes transfixed on each other, and they blew kisses to each other when their tongues weren't pressed hard together. It was passion and love as she whispered, "I will always love you, Trey, always."

Before he could respond, there was a hard knock at the front door. Simultaneously, they both jerked up wide-eyed. Candace tried to push Trey off, but he was stuck between passion and fear. "Trey, get off me," she hissed. Trey pulled back and out of her. She looked down to inspect herself. Seeing her blood scared her, but she was not too scared to forget that someone was at the front door.

"What are we going to do, Trey?" she asked.

"Put on your nightgown, and I'll see who's at the door," he whispered trying to appear in control. Slipping out of the room, Trey eased past the front door and peered through the curtains of the picture window. To his surprise, it was Candace's grandmother peering around in obvious annoyance.

Waking from the memory, Trey could only drop his head. He felt aroused even thinking about her. *I love you, Candace*, he thought. *Where are you? How could you do this to me, God!* his mind screamed.

೫೦೩೦೩

The Right Reverend never had his faith tested to this level. He didn't believe that his son was guilty, and he couldn't understand why this was happening.

Trey has a wild streak, but he's not a murderer. I've never seen any sign of this kind of violence. Trey wouldn't even handle my guns, and now he's accused of gunning down a human being. The thoughts racked his brain.

He remembered the day Trey was born, his first son. The doctor said he had never seen a father so happy and proud in his life. When Trey was an infant, they were inseparable.

"That's your child. He doesn't want anything to do with me when you're around. Give him to me, so I can breast-feed him unless you plan to do that too," his wife once said. She was a little upset but happy too. She loved the idea that she had brought something so wonderful into her husband's life.

The Right Reverend's mind returned to the present.

Were Trey's arrest and incarceration politically motivated? And then the thought hit him hard.

Could this be my fault?

The pain dropped him to his knees in prayer. After praying, he took a pen and paper and wrote to Trey.

My Dearest Son,

I have been a man of the cloth for most of my life. I have always reached out and advised others that they must have faith in the Lord. During their most difficult circumstances, I have told so many people that faith will show them the way. Now, I must take that advice for myself. My faith has never been tested to this level.

You are my son. I have nurtured you from your first steps and to your first years in college. I always thought I would be able to hold and protect you in all difficult and dangerous situations. I would give anything to hold you in my arms, in our own home, and to tell you I love you.

Today, you and I must believe in all I've preached. We must have faith. You are not alone. You have the love of your family and the generations that have gone before you. You have the love of a woman and your many friends. I know that your heart is heavy, and the world seems a terrible and desolate place.

I'm sure you question why this has happened to you. How can life be so cold and unfair? Where is God when I need him? The most tortured soul must find a way to see through the darkness to the blue horizon beckoning with greatness in the distance. God did not bring you in this world to waste you but for you to live and to grow in grace and power. God will look over you a thousand times and save you through each lonely night. You must see yourself as a gem becoming more valuable through each day's adversity. Please accept the words of this poem to lead you through these dark times and bring you to a place of redemption.

Destiny's Choice

Today I decide my future.
Which path will I choose?
The road less traveled or the path of least resistance?
Does my decision really matter?
Or, perhaps, everything is preordained?

My decision today will mirror the future,
Yet, since most decisions are not fixed.
My destiny is predicated at the point of decision,
And secured every day,
And every moment, the path is chosen.

Leaving the shelter of the nest,
I fear oblivion and contemplate soaring.
But is soaring a reflection of temporal success and security,
Or is it akin to stemming the torrential tides of life,
Thus courting oblivion?

Taking the less-traveled road
Portends pain, loss, and obstinate circumstances.
Whilst expedience may forestall the great consequences in life,
And afford the traveler immediate self-gratification,
It perchance condemns the follower to a rudderless path.

Biased, rugged terrain constricts the path to true love
And beckons loss into a slippery, black hole.
Yet, in survival, the lessons in faith, love, and devotion
Magnify and glorify the relationship,
Thus creating an unassailable bond.

Pain and trepidation are intrinsic to the thorny path
And, absence requisite,
Perhaps, leaving the child shoeless, wanton, and lonely.
Yet, the prickly lessons temper the child,
Preparing him for the great challenges in life.

Tears, bended back, blood,
And condemnation are the traveler's reward
For navigating steep, narrow grades and overgrown channels.
Yet, the path tempers the mind,
Strengthens the body, nourishes the soul,
And enlivens the spirit into an indomitable, impregnable force.

To struggle upstream against the undulating currents
Unveils character, perseverance, and desire.
It reveals belief in truth and justice,
Defeats the fear of spreading wings,
And affords the traveler his love, children, life, and soul.
It is our destiny and our choice.

Your Loving Father

CHAPTER TWELVE

"Tears, bended back, blood,
And condemnation are the traveler's reward,
For navigating steep, narrow grades and overgrown channels."

Trey knew this was his moment of truth. His first witness was Malik X. He had been an encouragement in prison had helped prepare Trey's case. He was polished and articulate. He contradicted and immediately compromised the body of evidence leveled by Gosselin. Trey introduced other inmates and institutional witnesses, including guards, and called prominent character witnesses who practically put the prosecution's case on life support.

Gosselin's cross-examinations showed a complete lack of preparation and knowledge of the case's intricacies. The judge and jury were enlivened, and the courtroom became animated. Everyone hung on Trey's words and actions. His presence became commanding. Trey had weathered the storm and basked in the glow of his day in court. As Trey watched the prosecution bungle another witness, his mind drifted, thinking, *Black October and my ultimate fate.*

ଓଝଓ

As usual, Sam Liddell, nicknamed Liddy, was sleeping late. Liddy loved the night and just wasn't a day person. Plus, his business was usually conducted under the cover of darkness. The telephone in his East Baltimore apartment rang sharply, and he reached to his nightstand to pick up the antique receiver. He smiled at the thought of the beautiful instrument and the knowledge that he had gotten a telephone worth three hundred dollars for a small packet of heroin.

Dumb-ass junkie, anything for a fix, he thought.

The telephone usually rang this time of day to give him a report on sales and problems encountered on the streets. He thought,

This Black October scare had slowed his sales recently, but a dopehead had to get his fix, and he would always be there to provide it.

"Hello," Liddy answered melodiously.

"Liddy, what's up, man? Long time no see. Look man, we've got to get together. I saw your boy Slim, and he says he wants to hook up," the voice on the other end said in a language only the two could decipher.

"How's Slim doing?" Liddy inquired.

"Slim's been better, and he told me to tell you that he needed to repay a favor."

"All right, I'll catch up with you later, and tell Slim I'll catch him at the club," Liddy responded succinctly.

"Later," came the final reply.

The message meant that heroin sales were going well, but the street supply was running low, and Liddy needed to resupply the street dealers as soon as possible. It also told him the drop-off location and that there were no major problems on the streets. Liddy lay back and smiled at the thought of turning over another supply of heroin, which meant sticking the big money in his pocket.

As he hung up the phone, he looked down at the thick white shag carpet in his bedroom and felt the cool of the red silk sheets on his back. A dark chocolate-colored thigh started sliding up his leg, and he turned his head to blow a kiss to the naked form beside him.

This was the life.

He'd worked his way up from a street dealer to having drug runners all over East Baltimore. He had increased his sales by putting under-aged kids to work, understanding that juveniles couldn't be given significant jail time. They rode bikes and scooters through the alleys and side streets of the city, and the cops couldn't really catch them.

The money was pouring in hand over fist, and he was virtually untouchable, passing the larger quantities onto the street to be broken down for his army of juvenile bikers. The Black October situation bothered him, but he couldn't imagine them nailing him because he wasn't on the streets.

Life was indeed sweet.

"Liddy. How about you sliding over here and rocking this girl's world?"

A sly grin appeared on her face. The darkness around her nipples accentuated her firm breasts and seemed an impossible color contrast to her dark skin tone. She seemed to be two colors, dark chocolate and black. The dark chocolate of her skin contrasted with the shocking flow of black hair on her head and the mound of black hair at the top of her thighs. He drank in the sight of her on his red silk sheets.

She was twenty years old and a ghetto flower. Most people didn't know that this kind of beauty existed in the despair of the inner city, but here it was.

Dee-Dee O'Connor loved the idea of Liddy's money and power. She felt safe from any harm with him and wanted everyone to know she was Liddy's girl. She knew Liddy controlled the heroin traffic in this part of East Baltimore. He was slim but very strong with powerful shoulders and chest muscles developed during his warring days on the streets of Charm City. He was five-foot-eleven inches tall and weighed a solid one hundred and seventy-five pounds. He had a six-pack stomach, which Dee-Dee strummed as if playing a tune. She playfully and slowly slid her fingers to the arising bulging member between his legs.

"Yeah baby, I want you bad."

Liddy rolled over and used his tongue to lick her neck before slowly moving up to flick at her full, juicy African lips.

"It's funny with you, babe. It's like I want you all over and everywhere at the same time."

Before he could do anything, Liddy was on his back, straddled and pinned by Dee-Dee's strong thighs. Her hands pinned his shoulders with token force as her breasts gently brushed against his chest and mouth. Her lips and tongue explored his neck, mouth, and tongue. After a long sensuous kiss, her tongue worked its way over his chin, around his neck, and down his chest and washboard stomach until her mouth ravenously engulfed his now-erect, throbbing member.

Liddy couldn't help thinking, *She always tries to please me.* Strangely, he wondered whether she truly loved him but then dismissed the thought when he acknowledged that he loved her.

It's crazy, he thought. I've never told her I love her, and I've always avoided any real statement of commitment. I've actually worked to confuse her about my emotions. I think that's going to change.

Liddy didn't want the rapture to climax without cloital penetration, and Dee-Dee was working hard and expertly to make him come.

He couldn't lie to himself anymore. He really had a tremendous passion for this woman.

He placed his hands under her face and gently guided her head off his aching dark chocolate penis.

"This is my problem, baby. I can't figure whether to kiss you all over or stick this thing in you right now."

"You're a big boy, Liddy. You'll figure it out," she said playfully.

"Yeah baby, this is going to be a la carte, and you're going to be the appetizer, entrée, and dessert."

Liddy plunged his head between her legs, ablaze with lust at the sweet aroma of her moist womanhood. He stayed there until he saw her hands were straining and clutching the silk sheets, almost tearing them from the bed.

Dee-Dee had the face of a super model. Her smooth, dark chocolate skin perfectly accentuated her sharp features, particularly her nose. Her large luscious lips seemed out of place on her slim face, but they were so functional. She was unusually well-endowed for a woman with such a slim frame. She believed in dressing in a way that did not show off her assets, often disguising her thirty-six-inch breasts and round juicy butt under flowing garments. Liddy appreciated her modesty in public and her wild abandon in bed. She seemed far more mature than her twenty years.

Liddy easily lifted Dee-Dee's five-foot-three-inch frame off the bed and, sitting back on his heels, lifted her onto his waiting and throbbing member. She let out a gasp as he penetrated savagely deep into her. Her feet were on the bed behind him, and her arms were around his neck. His hands firmly gripped her waist, allowing them both to control the flow of the sex.

The angle of their engagement allowed Liddy to kiss and to suck on her breasts and Dee-Dee to accommodate him. As the passion intensified, Liddy drove her back onto the mattress, fully spreading her legs to get maximum penetration. Their lovemaking became frantic, and they were lost in their world of ghetto passion.

Neither heard the sudden squeak door of the bedroom door as it partially opened.

Glimpsing at the dresser mirror, Liddy was surprised by the dark image he saw.

His mind rebelled, telling him to ignore it and concentrate on his shared passion with Dee-Dee, but his instincts told him to respond.

He concentrated and saw three camouflaged outfits emerge in stark contrast to the white carpet and red walls. With monumental force of will and to Dee-Dee's great surprise and dismay, Liddy bucked her off and lunged for his pistol in the nightstand.

The smirking Churchill quickly pounced on Liddy, violently clubbing him with the butt of his pistol.

In a deep baritone, he barked, "Get some clothes on that girl, and get her outta here."

Terror and shock registered on Dee-Dee's face but not a word escaped her mouth.

Liddy's mind was clouded from his throes of passion and the pain from the blow to his head.

Churchill and another camouflaged figure engulfed Liddy, swiftly taping his hands behind his back and roughly slapping more duct tape over his mouth. His renowned fighting prowess and super physique were of no use now.

"Get her outta here," Churchill snapped.

"If you open your mouth, you're dead," the third camouflaged figure said calmly, snatching the shocked naked girl out of the bed by her neck. As DeeDee was shoved toward the open bedroom door, Churchill yelled at Liddy.

"You are a known drug dealer, selling drugs in the black community. You are corrupting the young flowers of our community. You are compromising all our futures. These are acts of treason, and the penalty for treason is death."

"Get her dressed and outta here! Do I have to tell you again?" Churchill shouted to the third figure.

Dee-Dee was snatched by the arm and roughly pulled out of the bedroom.

As soon as the bedroom door closed, Churchill cut into Liddy with six silenced shots from a .38-caliber pistol. The muted shots thudded into Liddy's naked body, splattering blood on the wall behind his bed. The blood and gore on the white carpet and red silk sheets created a kaleidoscope effect in red and white design.

Churchill tossed leaflets over and beside the body.

By the time the men emerged from the bedroom, Dee-Dee was clothed in a white robe and tied to a chair with her mouth taped shut. Her eyes were wide, crazed, and terror-filled.

"It's time for you to grow up, and get your shit together," Churchill grabbed her face.

"We are Black October, and we want you to deliver a message to the police that they are holding the wrong man for the Connie Gordon execution.

"Tell them that the man they are holding is not, nor ever has been, a member of our organization. Tell them to check the ballistics against the bullets used on Connie Gordon and your late boyfriend here. Stay away from drug dealers!"

Minutes after Liddy was killed, Jerry picked up the ringing telephone at his office not far from the recent bloody execution.

"Hello."

"This is a member of Black October. A known drug dealer has just been killed in East Baltimore at the Avendale Apartments. He was shot in the chest six times with the same .38-caliber revolver that killed Connie Gordon. He has paid the price for pushing drugs. This should be enough evidence to prove that the police are holding the wrong man for the Connie Gordon execution. A young woman is under restraint in the apartment."

The line went dead, but Jerry's telephone immediately rang back.

"Mr. Freider, this is Sergeant Dempsey, Baltimore police. We were monitoring your call and intercepted and recorded your last message. Commander Bauer is being informed, and we are dispatching a team to the Avendale Apartments."

Jerry raced into Barry's office. He explained what happened, and immediately, there was a whirl of activity to identify the location of the Avendale Apartments. As soon as they were located, Jerry ran out of the office, heading to the reported crime scene. Again, he was concerned about going to East Baltimore, but he knew the police would be there first.

When he arrived, blue and white lights flashed off the apartment windows, and he saw a young woman being placed in a squad car. The car spun its wheels and took off like a shot. Other media reporters were on the scene, and the area was cordoned off.

Obviously, Black October had struck again.

Jerry was sure that the Ballards would hear about the latest murder and connect it with Black October.

Hopefully, this mess would give Trey some hope. If the murders continued like this, maybe the police would be forced to concede his innocence and release him. Anything's possible, Jerry thought.

Jerry's calls to Commander Bauer were not returned. There were no press conferences. The lid was now held tightly on the case. Jerry's pipelines went silent. He felt dead in the water. Not wanting to run afoul of Commander Bauer or *The Sun's* management, his next story was tempered with caution. He recounted the evidence and Trey's background. He introduced questions generated from the recent spate of murders and sought to raise doubts in Trey's favor.

A backlash grew against him at *The Sun*. He instinctively knew that any further straying from the company line would jeopardize his newfound front page by-line and deference.

His typewriter fell silent.

CHAPTER THIRTEEN

**"Yet, the path tempers the mind,
Strengthens the body, nourishes the soul,
And enlivens the spirit into an indomitable,
impregnable force."**

Jim Gosselin sat at the prosecution table remembering the tongue-lashing he'd taken. His boss had been direct and not pleasant at all. He remembered his stinging words.

"We give you the goose grease case of the century against an ignorant, untrained convict, and you have our case on life support."

Seeing his dreams dissipate and fearing the worst, Gosselin brought motions to suppress and to remove much of the defense's testimony. Trey was shocked and alarmed as he walked to the judge's chambers jabbering with his advocate.

"Can he do this? What recourse do I have? Hey, tell me something."

As soon as Gosselin entered the judge's chambers, he started screaming.

"His witness perjured himself by contradicting the testimony from his own trial and our discovery. Not only that, the institutional testimony should be thrown out because it's clearly prejudicial to my case."

With a condescending look, Judge Abrams replied, "Pump your brakes, counselor. You've gotten away with murder during this trial, and you know it. You brought in the institutional part, and I'm extending some latitude to the defendant to make his case. Now, Mr. Gosselin, take this as a warning. My courtroom is not a showplace for your agenda. If I find you going in that direction, I will hold you in contempt and slap a fine on you that you will not soon forget. All motions denied."

Trey tried to maintain his composure and suppress his glee. He pumped his fist as he walked back into the courtroom with a pimp in his step. Controlling his elation, he smiled thinking, *I've got a chance to win this thing. If I can win and get a new trial for the Gordon murder, I can get out of jail.*

ೞೞೞ

As soon as Churchill saw Butch, he let loose a tirade.

"Look, when I tell you to do something, do it! I told you to get her out of the bedroom, and you're fucking around looking at the girl's titties. You let her get a good look at us all."

Butch recoiled from the verbal onslaught and responded angrily.

"Hold ya horses, hoss! You seem to be forgetting who you talking to."

Churchill and Butch glared at each other. Finally, Churchill broke his iron gaze and looked down with pursed lips as he kicked at an imaginary object.

"I'm sorry, Butch."

Churchill's response broke the tension as they dapped and embraced. Butch left his hand on Churchill's shoulder and looked straight into his friend's eyes.

"Church, you and me been battling on the streets of Baltimore since we was hoppers. Everybody knows you were the leader of 'The Outlaws,' and a couple of other people know you were the King of Diamonds. I was down with you in 'Nam, and I'm down with you now. I slipped up with the girl, but you on edge, bro. I've never seen you like this before, my brother. You got to chill."

Churchill looked down again.

"Yeah, Butch, it's all getting to me, man. I don't know if we're getting anywhere, and we might be messing up. Trey's in jail, and we can't do a damn thing about it. He's like a little brother. He wasn't supposed to get caught up in this Black October shit, and now he's locked up for our shit."

"Yeah, Church, but we can't go haywire trying to clear Trey. You know the cops. They got to pin this shit on somebody, and, for whatever reason, Trey's the man. You can't control everything."

"Yeah man, but they know Black October's out there now. These fucking dope dealers are looking over their shoulders, and, like you said, if we knock off someone like Connie Gordon, it would be on, and it damn sure is. We got the police chief, the politicians, and the newspapers freaking out."

Laughing, Butch continued, "*The News American* even got us knocking off the minister who spoke over Gordon. They know we here now."

Looking up and nodding, Churchill said, "Yeah, the cops and dealers know we're here, and I don't know which is worse. Connie's boy up in New York is pushing up daisies. What's that about? We're making some very powerful people look bad and lose a lot of money. All we've done is pick up some chump change and possibly set ourselves up."

"Church, that's what I'm saying. We got to get rid of that .38 and the .45. If we get caught with them, we're up shit's creek. You know how niggas are. If anybody gets wind that we're Black October, they're gonna drop a dime. Then we either lock up with the dealers or the cops. We're sticking our necks out to save Trey, and we're exposed. He's got to stand his chances in court, and we got to stand down until this thing cools off."

"I hear you Butch, but I got to get Trey out of this mess. That boy was special to me. He's smart, tough, and he's got vision. Now, he's stuck in a hole."

Butch raised a finger to get Churchill's attention.

"Last thing on the subject of the girl, I wasn't staring at her tits. I was shocked because she looked just like your girl Ramona."

CHAPTER FOURTEEN

"To struggle upstream against the undulating currents,"

The jury hadn't missed Gosselin's comeuppance, and Trey noticed his approaches to the jury box were met with interest and acceptance. He ended the evidentiary part of his defense:

"Deputy Warden, at Lorton and until these allegations, was I ever reported to have perpetrated violence against anyone? Yes or no, please."

"No. We never had a reported problem with you."

"Thank you, Deputy Warden."

He looked at the jury, hunched his shoulders, and walked back to the defense table.

As Trey sat down, his second grasped his hand smiling.

"My compliments, Mr. Ballard, that was a brilliant defense. We got them on the ropes. You should be an attorney."

Trey smiled broadly and thanked him for the compliment and his assistance.

The words *You should be an attorney were infused in his mind.*

He thought, *Look at all the law books I studied at Lorton and the appeals, lawsuits, and writs I worked on for other inmates. Yes, I could be an attorney, but why am I here?*

Trey's mind drifted to Baltimore City Jail.

A baton jabbed Trey's spine, prodding him down a series of corridors. He passed steel doors with a single small window. Ultimately, he reached two tiers of cells with ten individual cells on each level. He was roughly pushed into the lower cell on the far end. As Trey turned to face the door, he heard it clank shut.

He dejectedly asked, "Can I get something to read?"

The guard snapped back, "Bring that up with your counselor," giving him a look that dismissed any further conversation.

Trey's cell included a barred window with a hazed-over view of a solid wall. It had a wooden bench for sleeping and a steel shelf with an attached wooden seat for eating. A steel-encased light barely illuminated the shelf. The only other fixture was a stark, lonely toilet.

A moth-eaten, threadbare blanket, a tiny, flimsy pillow, and a roll of toilet paper sat on the bed beside a rolled mattress. An inscription on the wall simply stated, "God Saves." Trey gulped in a deep breath and dropped to his knees in prayer. He didn't know if justice would prevail and sardonically laughed as he compared his modern-day situation to *Les Miserables*. The poem from his father was the only relief for him, and he recited it over and over in his mind. The pain of his incarceration and denial of bail had seeped into his soul.

೧೫೧೫೧೫

The Right Reverend sat with his face buried in his hands.

I'm certain that Trey is not guilty in this Black October mess. He thought back to the bloody days fighting for voting rights in Mississippi. *He'd been arrested, beaten, and falsely jailed because a redneck police officer said he matched the description of a robbery suspect.*

His confinement was laced with beatings under his armpits and behind his knees. There were late night interrogations and deprivation of food, water, and sleep. He was threatened and physically attacked at every turn. When the actual robber was arrested, he was freed but not before seeing the man dragged into the jail and beaten to a bloody pulp. The great irony was that in no imaginable way did the man bear any resemblance to him. He was a powerful man in Baltimore politics and greatly hated in certain circles. Would enemies attack Trey to silence me, and, if so, who are they?

The Right Reverend broke from his thoughts as his wife walked into the room. She sat beside him on the bed and waited quietly for him to speak.

"Bertha," came out as a deep croak. "I don't know what to make of any of this. I don't believe Trey's guilty and can only surmise that my enemies are behind it all. My heart is aching because I may have put our son in this jeopardy because of my politics."

Albertha pulled him close.

"I remember when he was a baby. He'd get out of his bed and put himself in front of the door until you came home. When you opened the door, you would tap and awaken him. Then he wouldn't leave your side until he went to sleep at night. I always said he was your child."

The Right Reverend smiled.

"You know he would even stand at the bathroom door until I came out."

The Right Reverend's mind temporarily drifted to the thought of a Sunday sermon, but the thought evaporated as quickly as it emerged. He thought of how he desperately wanted a son and the fear that accompanied that wish. He knew that the society did not favor black boys. Many theories had been espoused as to why black boys were targets in America. There were the sexual dominance, racial dissolution, and intimidation theories. Maybe Trey's circumstance involved a little of each, but it didn't matter now. My son is a victim, and I can't come to his rescue.

As the Right Reverend finished his recriminations, he turned to his wife.

"Bertha, we've got to get that boy out of jail."

ଔଔଔ

The next day, Kenneth L. Jones sat across from the Right Reverend and tried to be as delicate and diplomatic as possible.

"Reverend Ballard, I'm generally against trying cases in the press or public eye. Plus, I believe there are personal or political dimensions to this case."

The Right Reverend fired back. "Are you saying this is directed against me?"

Jones's hands shot up in a defensive posture.

"No, no, Reverend. That is not my point. I am completely focused on the best approach to exonerate your son."

The Right Reverend retorted, "Mr. Jones, that is why we need a proper public outcry to move the courts in favor of my son. The churches and civil rights groups want to organize massive rallies and demonstrations. We can put some fire under these folks."

Jones dejectedly replied, "Reverend, the trial is looming, and we're not getting any cooperation or movement from the prosecution. We are losing valuable time. By the time the demonstrations are organized and launched, they'll have already convicted Trey."

The Right Reverend's eyes narrowed.

"Look, Mr. Jones, you were hired for your legal expertise. I, on the other hand, have responsibility to the church and the civil rights groups that have put money up for Trey's defense. I've promised a third of the funds to work to change laws governing the arrest of young black males and for feeding the hungry."

Exasperated, Jones breathed deeply.

"Reverend Ballard, we need to stay focused on your son, this case, and this case alone."

The Right Reverend angrily snapped back.

"Mr. Jones, you are supposed to be the best attorney available. They only have circumstantial evidence. You have a mountain of evidence to exonerate my son. You've got questions about the gun. You've got Black October claiming to have committed the murders. You've got character witnesses, and you're the best at deflating the prosecutors' inflated evidence. If you just make it appear circumstantial, I'm sure we can win."

Jones dropped his head and paused to defuse any further argument.

"Reverend Ballard, I have been working this case legally and behind the scenes. There is an ugly undercurrent coming from somewhere. They won't relent on bail, charges, venue, or time. They are directed and relentless. I've only seen this happen once before, and the outcome was not good. Something or someone very powerful is driving this prosecution. To succeed, we have to put forward a perfect case. The funds must be used for juror selection analysis, investigations, forensics, witness preparation, and, let's say, flexibility in putting our case forward."

The Right Reverend indignantly shot back.

"Flexibility? What kind of flexibility are you talking about Mr. Jones?"

"Reverend Ballard, I have been in this business for decades, and I've seen things in courtrooms you would not believe. Please do not ask me to explain how we get our work done, but I'll tell you this. Sometimes you have to fight fire with fire and ugly with ugly. Do what you must with the money, Reverend. I'll follow your lead by talking with someone in the press that might be a friend. Let's get this done."

⋘⋙

Candace and the Right Reverend sat across from the Plexiglass window and watched Trey move deliberately toward his chair. He appeared gaunt and dark circles ringed his eyes. As Trey took his seat, the guard took several steps back but stayed within earshot. Trey picked up the telephone and placed his hand on the clear barrier opposite Candace's.

The Right Reverend picked up the telephone first as Trey and Candace stared into each other's eyes. His heart tugged seeing the lovers' separation, but knew his job was to give his son hope.

"Trey, how are you, my son?" he asked cheerily.

"I'm surviving, Dad, but this has been pretty rough. How's mom, Brenda, and Clifton?" Trey asked finally looking in his father's direction.

"Son, everyone's fine. We just miss you. We're gonna get you home soon. The church and the civil rights groups are working hard to publicize your case. Kenneth Jones has been retained as your lawyer. That group Black October is professing your innocence and apparently providing contradictory evidence in your favor. Be of faith, son. God's on your side. I believe this has more to do with my politics and me than anything you've done."

Trey's hand never left its position opposite Candace's, but he responded quickly.

"Dad, you've always been a man of conviction, strength, and

integrity. If this is visited on me because of your convictions, then it shows you're doing something necessary and right. I wouldn't exchange you for any father on earth."

The Right Reverend wiped at his eyes and passed the telephone to Candace.

"Thank you. Be strong." He nodded firmly and stepped away with his head bowed.

Trey looked into Candace's eyes.

"Well, the last time we talked I was supposed to call you the next day."

Candace's tears flowed, and Trey noticed the quiver of her lips.

"Candace, you know I love you. The only thing I want is to marry you and have a million children. If I've learned anything from this nightmare, I now know never to take anything for granted, especially you. If God should show me a way out of this mess, I'll never be far from you again. I'll swear that on a stack of Bibles."

Candace forced the words from her mouth.

"Trey, I can't believe this is happening. I can't stand the idea of you being in jail and our being apart. I worry about you all the time. What's going to happen? Look, I'm supposed to be encouraging you, and I'm a mess."

Trey smiled legitimately for the first time since his arrest.

"I'm looking at the woman I love, and you're far from a mess. This barrier is our only impediment and even that's transparent. I'll come back to you sweetie. I will come back."

☙❦☙

Kenneth Jones hit his intercom button. "Yes?"

"Mr. Jones, there's a Mr. Jerry Freider for you."

"Thank you Gladys. Send him right in please." Jones rose from behind his desk and quickly walked to shake hands.

"Mr. Freider, thank you for coming on such short notice. It's a pleasure to meet you."

"Same to you, sir," Jerry said as his eyes scanned Jones's

plush corner office. *Maybe I'm in the wrong business.*

"Mr. Freider"

Jerry quickly stopped Jones.

"Please, it's Jerry. Mr. Freider's my dad."

Jones replied smiling. "Jerry it is. I'm Kenneth Jones."

Jerry stopped Jones again.

"Sir, everyone knows who you are. You're one of the most prominent lawyers in Baltimore."

Jones nodded to Jerry. "Call me Kenny, and, speaking of fathers, mine always said that it's good to be important but more important to be good."

They laughed and shook hands again.

"Jerry, can I get you some coffee or a drink?"

Jerry grinned slyly.

"Can you make it a Jack and Coke?"

Jones smiled back. "Only if I can join you."

Minutes later, they sat across from each other chatting and nursing their drinks.

"Jerry, as you know, I'm representing Ballard in the Black October case, and I want to congratulate you for your insightful reporting. As a matter of fact, I'm getting more information from your articles than from the prosecutor's office."

Jerry studied Jones as he sipped his drink. "Thank you, sir. It's kind of you to say."

"Now Jerry, I know you're a busy man, so I'll be direct. I believe you favor my client and think he's innocent."

Jerry lifted his glass.

"I'll take the fifth on that one, sir," smiling at his pun.

The defense attorney followed suit by taking another sip.

"Well okay, let's say I go on the premise that I have information to contribute to your stories and trust that you will present it fairly."

Jerry calmly answered, "That's my job."

"Jerry, I'm not getting anywhere with the prosecutor or his office on this case. My private client-lawyer exchanges have been compromised. I've been denied access to key evidence, including ballistics and autopsy reports. For instance, I asked for a copy of the police affidavit for the Ballards' search and seizure warrant but was told that copies were not available. I'm filing all the proper motions and running into brick walls."

Jerry put on his reporter face.

"What do you want from me, sir?"

Jones leaned back in his red leather chair, his face lined in concentration.

"Jerry, I think the public needs to know the problems we're facing. The skids for this kid's conviction have been greased. My contacts aren't returning my calls, and the honest officials can't look me straight in the eye. I'm suggesting that you need to think in terms of who's driving this prosecution against Ballard and why. I think it's coming from on high, very high. We need the press to even the playing field."

"Let me be perfectly honest with you. I'm walking a tightrope at *The Sun* trying to adhere to the company line. My last article was not well received, and I've fallen off the front page and may be fading fast. To be perfectly honest, my options are limited."

Jerry's next story stated Jones's allegations and directed attention to the staff and workings of the prosecutor's office. He suggested that Trey's prosecution was aggressive and not necessarily warranted. Though Jerry's story was heavily edited, the essence of the message came through.

State's Attorney Hilton faced microphones on the steps of the courthouse.

"Mr. Jones was not denied documents entitled to the defense. The state maintains that Mr. Ballard is a menace to society. The fear instilled by Black October makes it imperative to continue his denial of bail. There is no conspiracy or special prosecution coming from this office."

It was in this atmosphere that the Black October murder trial began against Trey. The problems with the defense fund escalated and compromised Jones's defense. Key evidence continued to be denied, and Jones couldn't seem to get a motion passed. To no one's surprise, the trial went badly, and Trey was convicted.

As the jury filed out, officers attached restraints from Trey's waist to his hands and feet. With a wry smile, he turned to look at Candace and his family and then dropped his head while awkwardly shuffling out of the courtroom.

☙❦❧

"Governor, regarding the Ballard conviction, we just received a request from his Congressional district to allow him to serve his sentence at a minimum security institution. Shall we comply?"

Cigar smoke drifted in the air as the rotund figure swung in his chair, exhibiting the glee of a child on a merry-go-round. He laughed deeply and smiled, giving a thumbs-up to the huge picture of Gerald Ford hanging between the American flags behind his desk.

The Governor of Maryland had an answer.

"To hell with that sanctimonious son-of-a-bitch preacher and his whelp. Let his son go to Lorton or somewhere out of this area. Just don't let it be a country club prison. Hopefully, this will shut him up along with those other fools in Baltimore. They'll think twice before playing politics with me."

CHAPTER FIFTEEN

"Unveils character, perseverance, and desire."

The Lorton trial had been a rollercoaster ride for Trey, and he felt on top for the moment. He knew that Gosselin would pull out all stops to take back the advantage. Trey willed himself to concentrate. Gosselin rose from his seat and pulled on the lapels of his charcoal-gray Brooks Brothers suit. He leveled his head, so his Adam's apple would fall into line with the top button of his heavily starched, white, buttoned-down shirt. He marched directly to the jury box and paraded in front of the jurors like a drill sergeant in front of raw recruits. After making eye contact with each juror, he jerked a pointed finger at Trey blurting out:

"This man is guilty of arson and criminal conspiracy to riot at Lorton. He is a convict with a criminal predisposition."

He continued his march, raising his voice.

"Prominent witnesses have placed this man in a planning meeting preceding the riot. He was also identified as a participant in the riot itself."

Jerking his hands skyward, he said in a heavily sarcastic tone, "There is nothing more that you need to convict.

"Is this man a model citizen? No, he's in jail for conspiracy. Is he a person you would want wandering through your neighborhood? No. Is he part of the Occoquan community? No. He's been imported from the urban jungle to wreak havoc on all we hold near and dear.

"Today I ask you to convict this man. No, I demand a conviction for your own safety. We must send a clear and unambiguous message to all the inmates in Lorton and to the criminals in Washington D.C. that Virginia is not a playground for violent criminals. That message must be firm and resolute. Thank you, ladies and gentlemen."

As Gosselin finished his closing argument, he turned and gave a disgusted look in Trey's direction before sauntering back to his chair.

Trey noticed Judge Abrams fidgeting behind the bench.

Maybe she's concerned about my close, he thought. For whatever reason, she favors me. Maybe she's thinking I'll make a spectacle of her courtroom and myself. I can't let that happen. I must be great and reach the jury from within. Be professional and, above all, be human.

Trey summoned all his strength to force himself to relax. He conferred with his second, trying to appear polished, professional, and composed. It had been a long road from his arrest in Baltimore to this trial. But, for some reason, Trey's mind focused on Churchill.

Trey smirked, envisioning Gosselin alone with Churchill. Gosselin would probably piss his pants. It had been years since Churchill had been his protector and surrogate big brother. Nevertheless, he still felt a strong kinship and brotherhood. Now a man in his own right, Trey would love to see and talk to Churchill man to man.

ଔଔଔ

"Goldie, we got a problem," Murph pleaded.

"Our smack supply is next to nothin'. The Connie connection is gone. We was getting shit from Liddy on the eastside. Now dat's gone. Now we can't get shit from nobody. Nobody knows who to trust no more. You got that two-grand bounty out for information on Black October, and we ain't heard a peep. If I ain't mistaken, dis still B-more, and you can buy a nigga for five bucks. The cops jammed our main nigga the other night, and now he screaming on me."

Speaking slowly, he continued, "Goldie, dis was a joke until Liddy got blown away. That was a bad-ass nigga. Ain't nobody walking up on him. Yuh hear me!"

Again, Murph paused for effect, speaking each word slowly.

"Goldie, whoever knocked off Liddy has got to be a real bad motherfucker."

Murph's last statement caused Goldie to sit up straight.

"What?" Murph asked when he saw his boss's reaction.

Goldie smiled, laced his fingers, and sat back rocking and twisting in his lounge chair. Golden lights danced off Goldie's gold-plated smile.

"Murph I need you and a couple of the boys this evening. Make it around six o'clock. I got some things to do right now. See ya later."

Murph shook his head, exhaled deeply, and replied, "Alright boss."

He wanted to say more but thought better of it and exited quickly, shaking his head all the way.

Thomas "Goldie" Walker controlled the heroin traffic on the lower westside of Baltimore City. He picked up the nickname Goldie after he put gold caps on the entire top row of his teeth. Conspicuous consumption was important to Goldie, so he had to have more gold teeth than anyone, which was no small feat in Baltimore.

He'd built his empire on ruthless execution. He rarely had competition and knew what to do if he found it. He frowned when he thought about somebody killing Romy other than him.

If it weren't for the warnings directly from the cops, I would've ventilated Romy's brain myself for even thinking he could operate on my territory.

Something Murph said made this Black October situation fit together. Murph was right. It had to be a bad motherfucker to take out Liddy. Also, it had to be someone who knew how to run a secret operation in Baltimore. Even punk-ass Romy's killing fit the pattern. I'd bet my life I know the main clue to the puzzle.

Goldie's elation over his epiphany dissipated quickly with a sinking feeling of trepidation. Gritting his teeth and slowly shaking his head side to side, he thought: *Well it looks like me and my old homeboy going to have a little talk.*

☙❧

Placing a cold rag on his forehead, Churchill fell straight back onto the sofa in Ramona's basement. He stared at the ceiling thinking, *What next and what about Trey?*

Everything's out of control. I wanted to make a statement with Black October, but I'm feeling no satisfaction. Me and the other vets are no better off. We're not getting jobs making legit money, and people are dying. Worse, Trey is languishing in jail for my deeds.

Ramona slowly and seductively slid onto the sofa while pulling Churchill's arm around her. She burrowed her head deep into the nook between his head and neck. Her soft body melted onto his muscular frame, and she gently stroked his face. He loved these moments with Ramona, feeling they were the perfect physical fit. No music or television diluted their shared connection and many times, like now, they would not speak.

They lay in silence until Ramona began to whisper:

"Church, I'm worried. You don't seem like yourself lately, and all this Black October stuff is giving me the creeps. I know you don't want to hear this, but I think they killed Romy. If they killed him, they might kill you. I can't lose you, Church."

Ramona's words broke their comfortable body connection. Restless, Churchill sat up on the sofa. He took a deep breath and pulled Ramona close, kissing her deeply for over a minute.

When their lips parted, he said, "Sweetie, I love you more than I can say, and I know you feel it when things aren't right with me. I told you that Trey's a little brother to me, and I'm worried about him. As far as Black October knocking me off, don't even think about that. I'm not dealing dope, and I can take care of myself."

Ramona broke from his arms and stood.

"Church, do you know who's in Black October?"

Churchill's mind panicked, but he answered quickly.

"Don't grit on me like that, Mona. That's dangerous talk. So just let it go now."

Ramona was the first woman to get this close to him. *No matter how much I love her, I can't have her thinking like this, much less ex-*

pressing it. He had long been rumored to be the King of Diamonds but that could always be played off as an urban legend. Killing Romy was something he could never tell her. He felt fear for the first time since Vietnam.

Churchill saw Ramona's lips quivering, wanting to speak. He looked deeply in her eyes trying to determine what to say.

A minute before was fine. Now I have to say the right thing.

He wanted to be the tower of strength that everyone perceived the great Churchill Harding to be, but now he was just a man with the woman he loved.

As Churchill drank in Ramona's great beauty, his heart melted before her little girl's vulnerability. Ramona was the epitome of beauty to him, and she had made a goddess-like imprint on his mind. He wanted to trust her completely, but having no experience with love, he didn't know what to do. Her dark chocolate skin was like that DeeDee, the girl at Liddy's. Their thick lips and full, firm breasts were almost identical. He remembered Butch's statement about their resemblance.

They did look alike. Maybe my verbal attack on Butch was as much about the association of the women as anything.

Finally, he said, "Look Mona, I've got some serious stuff to do, and I gotta run."

"Where ya going, Church?" came her high-pitched reply. "You just gonna walk out now? Church, I got a bad feeling about this Black October stuff. I don't want you out now."

Churchill smiled at her concern for his safety.

"Mona, when I get back, we'll sit down and talk seriously about our future. Stop," Churchill held up his hand to stop her from speaking.

"Look, I love you. I'm going to be with you forever. We're getting married and having little Churchills and Monas, but now I got to leave and work something out. So, I'm walking out now, but I'll be back in a minute. When I get back, we'll talk. I think it's time to say goodbye to Harlem Avenue."

Churchill kissed Ramona and left quickly. He skipped up the basement steps two at a time. He didn't want a confrontation with

Ramona, especially one he couldn't win. As he hit the street, a late afternoon breeze splashed his face, giving him a momentary respite from the myriad thoughts dominating his mind. The sky was partly overcast with floating gray clouds against a dull blue background. The cool breeze was intermittent as the sun moved from behind the clouds, giving a taste of the lingering summer heat. It had been a hot summer in more ways than one.

He had to talk to the people he could trust, and his steps guided him to the neighborhood gathering spot above Evergreen Park. Butch was already there swigging on a bottle of lime Flip. The other boys were sharing bottles of Thunderbird and Wild Irish Rose.

Butch extended the bottle of cheap wine in his direction.

"Church, where ya been?" Laughing and looking at the others, he said, "As if we don't know."

Churchill good-humouredly replied, "Ramona's fine and no wine for me. Watch that stuff, Butch. It may taste like fruit juice, but the lead in it is going to rot your brain and eat your liver."

Butch listed to the side as he lifted the pint of wine in the air saying, "Church, I need a good buzz."

"Yeah man, I know," Churchill responded solemnly. He had always been a decisive person, and he knew instinctively that this was a serious and critical timeframe. He still didn't know what to do and needed his most trusted allies now.

"Butch, give that shit to somebody else. We got to talk."

Butch gave a hiccup laugh and turned the bottle upward, draining it to the last drops. Finishing it, he belched. "Man, I used my last ducats on that thing, and I ain't giving it away."

Churchill shook his head with a sardonic laugh, "Come on, man. I've got some ends, and we got to talk."

Butch was on his feet quickly. "Ends? Let's go."

Churchill grabbed Butch's arm to steady him, drawing a drunken smile from his lieutenant.

"Let's walk up to Dave's. I'll buy you a Coke to dilute the lead you been drinking."

Churchill led Butch up Harlem Avenue, making a left onto Ashburton Street. He briefly chastised himself for retracing his steps. He felt this was a sign of inefficiency and poor planning, two things he couldn't afford now. His first order of business was to get Butch back in his right mind. Secondly, he had to sit down with the brains of the operation.

Churchill purchased a Coke for Butch at Dave's, and together they made a left on Edmondson Avenue and walked down the hill toward Evergreen Park. He laughed to himself, thinking about Trey walking up the hill in his drawers from the trolley incident.

That was the third order of business, what to do about Trey.

Soon they reached a house on the opposite side of Evergreen Park. They could actually look back and see their homeboys in the distance still drinking wine. The homes on this side of the park were not the classic Baltimore row homes with white marble steps. They were semi-detached colonials with fully manicured front and back lawns. They were beautiful, truly flowers in the middle of a ghetto desert.

Churchill rang the doorbell and listened as he heard footsteps approach.

"Georgie, what's up Negro?"

Churchill smiled, stepping into the vestibule to hug his friend. Butch followed his lead.

"Come in, come in." Joy emanated from George.

"Sit down. Can I get you something from the kitchen?"

Butch belched from the Coke he had just downed and slurred his words. "Coke on ice for me."

George chuckled. "Butch, I keep telling you about drinking that sneaky-pete wine. You need to leave that stuff alone."

George had the ability to minimize the bad and accentuate the good in most situations, effectively turning a sow's ear into a silk purse.

"Coke for me too, Georgie," Churchill said, smiling at the shared advice.

George Hamm was what Churchill and the Harlem Avenue homeboys called a "cross-the-park-boy." He was part of the neighborhood, and then again he wasn't. George wasn't one of the neighborhood toughs nor did he roughhouse in the park with the rest of the guys. He wasn't tall or ripped with muscle. He was just the opposite. As a child, George had survived the trauma of open-heart surgery. Instead of roughhousing in the park, he endured numerous doctor visits and hospital stays. He'd told Churchill about his heart surgery saying, "The only thing worse than the operation was going through the lengthy recovery."

George knew about business, social issues, and how to work political agendas. He'd already successfully campaigned for two prominent Baltimore government officials.

George and Churchill could take a specific point and delve into its political and social ramifications for hours. They often analyzed how Baltimore could find itself among the world's leaders in consumption of expensive alcoholic beverages and drugs.

They asked, "Where was this kind of money coming from in a depressed and predominantly blue-collar city like Baltimore?" When they talked, they didn't just look at the point but looked for solutions. That's why Churchill was there. He needed the greatness of George's mind.

Churchill smiled as he likened himself, Butch, and George to the legendary crime trio of Meyer Lansky, Lucky Luciano, and Bugsy Siegel. Obviously, he was Lucky, and Butch was Bugsy, but most people did not realize the importance of George, their version of Meyer Lansky.

Smiling, George returned with a tray, setting the bottles of Coke and ice-filled glasses in front of Churchill and Butch. George's red paisley ascot coordinated perfectly with his red smoking jacket and black lounge pants. George projected an air of aristocracy, and, if you didn't know better, you'd think you were in a study with Rex Harrison. George sat, sinking upright into his red leather chair.

"Gentlemen, what can I do for you today?"

Churchill poured the brown liquid over the ice and watched the beige foam shoot to the lip of the glass. Waiting for the foam to settle, he looked up.

"Look, Georgie, we got to shut Black October down. It's completely out of control. We're like in Vietnam with no clear-cut mission and no end game. Our end game at this point is everybody dead, if not from the cops, then dead economically and mentally.

Trey's in jail, and we knocked off people trying to show the cops they don't have the right man. It hasn't helped, and we've reached a dead end. More important than anything, my heart is just not in this anymore. I never imagined my feelings for Ramona would grow to this level, and now I just want to be with her and build a life around her. I think it's time for me to get out of Baltimore."

George's fingers were laced, and his eyes peered over the top of his intertwined hands. He listened intently and observed all of Churchill's body mechanics as he spoke. He paused to let Churchill's words hang in the air. He was not worried about Butch interjecting because he rarely spoke when the two brains communicated.

Finally, George dropped his hands to his lap and cleared his throat:

"Church, you've been warring with 'The Outlaws' and 'The Diamonds,' and in Vietnam, and now it's Black October. I'm glad to hear what you've said. Now, whatever move you make has to include Butch. I'll be fine. I'm confident you're big enough to make a place for both of you."

Churchill explained, "Right now, other than Trey, none of our people have been indicted or to my knowledge even suspected. The pressure is only going to grow because the police, especially Commander Bauer, want a scapegoat real bad. Bauer's got his professional and street reputation on the line. Don't forget Connie was a delegate, and his execution has federal implications, which means the FBI may be investigating, and it does have black agents."

George continued, "Plus, let's not forget the dealers. They have a lot of pull, and vengeance can come from anywhere. You damaged their drug pipelines and clearly decreased their sales. The ramifications of these events are reverberating up and down the Northeast corridor. WeeWee, who was hooked up with Connie, got shanked in prison. It wasn't the cops that ordered that, and it wasn't an accident. The drug boys are not happy, and they are more likely than the cops or the FBI to tie this to us."

"I completely agree with you," he continued. "We have no end game. In this situation, sometimes it's best to cut your losses and run. We've been fighting a form of guerrilla warfare, which has six basic principles: the objective, speed and surprise, momentum, resupply, security, and exit strategy. We've done well in all areas except the last three. Above all else, we must have an effective exit strategy.

"I've been giving this a lot of thought," George added, clearing his throat.

"I believe it's time you, Butch, and Ramona get outta here. I suggest Mexico. I'm going to set you up to go to Cozumel. You'll have passports and a basic itinerary. You'll be close to the Texas border and the Caribbean side of Mexico. The area is surrounded on three sides by jungle, which I'm sure you boys can use to your advantage. The fourth side is open-ocean, which can be a good escape option if you start feeling any pressure. That move will definitely take you out of the mix. I've got the ends we've saved, and I'll start getting things together for your move. I think you'll like it there and do well."

০৪০৪০৪

Butch and Churchill decided to take the long way home rather than cut straight back across the park.

As they walked up Edmondson Avenue toward Evergreen Park, a gleaming, gold Lincoln Continental Mark IV pulled ahead of them and parked. It had all the standard gangster accoutrements, extra wide whitewall tires, trimmed spoke hubcaps, and a diamond-shaped rear window, all uniquely trimmed in gold.

"I'm packing, Church," Butch quickly stated.

Going on high alert, Churchill responded, "Good, at least one of us is on point. I don't have anything on me, so if something jumps off, spray 'em, and get to the park the best way you can."

Goldie stepped from the rear passenger side of the Lincoln and extended his arms. He spun in place to show he didn't have a gun and to display his outfit. He wore an off-white leisure suit with matching Dan Brother gator shoes. His white fedora had a gold headband to match his gold-trimmed sunglasses. Light from the overhead streetlamp reflected off the gold jewelry on his neck, fingers, and teeth.

The windows of the vehicle were darkly tinted, and Churchill was sure he wasn't alone.

"Church, my nig-ga," Goldie drew out nigga for almost two seconds. "Long time no see."

With an icy stare, Churchill replied, "Yeah, what's up, Goldie? You know I don't appreciate nobody pulling up on me."

"Yeah Church, but I want to have a quick, private talk wit you."

Churchill responded by waving his right hand to an area a few feet away.

"Okay Goldie, step into my office."

Goldie pimped to the place Churchill designated and spun like a runway model to face him. The show infuriated Churchill, but he didn't let it show. Instead, he gave Butch a silent command to watch his back and to stay positioned between him and the car.

At least the 'Nam training was good for something, he thought.

Goldie preened with his eyes cast down. Then he looked up. "Look Church, I ain't gonna beat around the bush."

Controlling his anger, Churchill replied in a dry, cutting tone, "That would be good, Goldie."

Savoring his words, Goldie continued.

"You know Church, I been thinking about dis Black October stuff, and only a few niggas in this town that could pull dis off. Only a bad-ass nigga with some serious street time and connections could do dis. It would take a nigga like you, Church."

"Is that right?" Churchill continued his dry tone, masking his alarm. "Maybe it's somebody from out of town, huh?" he added flatly.

Dismissing Churchill's statement, Goldie responded as he pretended to dust off the lapels of his suit.

"I doubt that, Church. 'Cuz this is still B-more, and niggas just don't come walking up into dis camp. You know dat like me. Now, Church, all dis Black October shit is hurting my business and costing me plenty money."

Icily, Churchill continued his flat response.

"That sounds like a personal problem to me, Goldie."

Now, insolent, Goldie raised his voice.

"Okay Church, enough of dis horse shit! Either you part of dis Black October shit or you know who is. One way or the other, it's a problem to me."

"Well, what you want to do, Tommy?" Churchill challenged Goldie by using his real name to reinforce his contempt for the man.

"Yeah Tommy, I remember when your mama would beat your ass and run you home in those fish-head tennis shoes. If you think getting a bunch of gold teeth in your mouth means anything to me, you dreaming. You walk up on me talking shit. You know who the fuck I am, not to mention the pull I got."

Goldie was irate, spittle sailing from his wide mouth in all directions.

"Tommy! Tommy! Who the fuck you calling Tommy, motherfucker? I'm Goldie, goddamn bad-ass Goldie, and if you--"

Goldie didn't get another word out of his mouth before Churchill hit him with a vicious punch below his nose and above his two front teeth. Goldie seemed to shrug, twist, and freeze from the impact of the blow. He collapsed straight down, dropping hard to the pavement.

Butch pulled his gun, but concealed it by his side, and Churchill reached to the small of his back pretending to finger a weapon. Three figures spilled from the car with hands on unexposed guns. They were at Goldie's side in an instant.

Churchill whispered, "You first, Tommy."

Blood from Goldie's mouth streamed between his fingers, but he managed to scream to his men:

"No, no, not here! Not here!"

It was a Mexican standoff, with the advantage to Churchill's reputation and proximity to Evergreen Park.

The men helped Goldie to his feet. As Goldie looked down, he saw two small, gleaming objects at his feet.

"You knocked my teeth out, nigga."

Contemptuously, Churchill looked down at the teeth and then directly into Goldie's eyes.

"Yeah, pick 'em up, and get the fuck outta here."

Goldie hissed a gap-toothed warning as his men hustled him to his car.

"Alright motherfucker, remember dis. 'Member dis!"

Butch hurried to Churchill's side saying, "Damn, Church, what was up with dat?"

Churchill replied slowly and deliberately, "Well, the shit's hit the fan now. He suspects me of being in Black October. He got smart with me, and I decided to dust him off. Plus, his fashion sense insulted me. Like Ramona taught me, anybody who wears white after Labor Day is a coon."

Butch exhaled, shaking his head from side to side.

"Wheew, Church, one thing's for damn sure, being around you, there's never a dull moment."

Churchill commanded with the authority of a general.

"All jokes aside. Let's get back to George's, quick!"

CHAPTER SIXTEEN

**"It reveals belief in truth and justice,
Defeats the fear of spreading wings,"**

Trey's second rushed into the courtroom and plopped next to him. Excitedly, he whispered in Trey's ear.

"Mr. Ballard, Gosselin wants to discuss a plea bargain. We should consider it because he's got his entire political future tied up in this case."

Laughing, Trey replied, "That nimrod, a leader of the people? I'd rather rot in hell before helping him do anything. Tell him to forget it. Of course, be polite, legally correct, and thank him profusely."

Trey sat back and smiled.

Gosselin was nervous and obviously for good reason. He knew Gosselin could care less about him or Lorton.

He thought of his father's poem, "Taking the less-traveled road portends pain, loss, and obstinate circumstances."

I'll take the obstinate road and pray that it leads me everywhere.

His mind drifted to thoughts of finality and deliverance. He thought of Black October.

ಠಠಠ

Commander Bauer had trouble focusing his questions because of Dee-Dee's beauty.

Boy I'd like to jump those bones with her boyfriend out of the way now.

"You've got to be able to tell us something else about the men who came into Liddell's apartment," Bauer pressed in a warning tone.

She is definitely not like the scarecrow-looking heroin hags I'm used to seeing here. No, this girl is a stunning beauty with a great body. I've got the nagging feeling I met her before. Can't place it now, but my intuition is usually correct. The connection will come to me.

Bauer had to get the police commissioner off his back. He'd run as much shit downhill as possible, and the onus was now on him. A press conference was scheduled for the afternoon, and he was hoping to get a break from Dee-Dee on the Black October case. That's why he was re-interviewing her, or did he just want to see her again? Every time he saw her, her beauty struck a nerve. But now he had to get ready for the press conference.

ଔଔଔ

Goldie stared in the mirror at the bloody gap where his two front teeth had been.

"I'm going to git that motherfucker if it's da last thing I do! I'm going to blow that son-of-a-bitch away!" he screamed and ranted violently, nearly out of control.

One of Goldie's men said, tempering his words, "Goldie, you got to think about taking Churchill head on. We can't walk up on Harlem Avenue. That would be like Custer's last stand."

Goldie cut venomous eyes at his man who recoiled in fear, but the message sank in, making Goldie plop into his chair. Finally he said, "We got to draw Churchill out."

ଔଔଔ

Commander Bauer approached the podium containing a phalanx of microphones. In front of the podium was a table stacked with weapons, money, and drugs.

Smiling, he began, "Twenty arrests in the sting dubbed Operation Zero Tolerance were made Thursday in the Eastern and Western districts of the city. Along with the arrests, officers seized 22 firearms, 21 pounds of marijuana, two kilos of heroin, and one hundred and fifty thousand dollars in cash. Federal, state, and local law enforcement agencies participated in the sting, and more arrests are pending.

"This is the first step in our zero tolerance policy. Baltimore will no longer be a free trade zone for drugs. Rest assured, we will be relentless in targeting drug traffickers and their illicit gains. We will take away their money and drugs."

Commander Bauer stood back and smiled for the cameras. Unlike earlier press conferences, he opened the floor for questions. He pointed to Jerry for the first question.

"Commander Bauer, congratulations on this sting. How does this coincide with the Black October investigation? It seems you are both saying the same thing at this point."

Bauer turned red-faced as he stared at Jerry with evil intent. Trying to suppress his mounting anger, he said, "Mr. Freider, the Black October investigation is continuing, and we have some promising developments."

"Like what?" Jerry popped off. Jerry's question set off a feeding frenzy from the other press.

They completely ignored Bauer's arrest report and honed in on Black October. After several minutes of intense, pointed questioning, Bauer stalked away from the podium.

☙❧☙

"Butch, get back across the park fast, and tell the boys what happened. Get them ready, and call me back here," Churchill said, barking out orders.

"Got you, Church," Butch replied, quickly dashing out the door.

George started slowly. "Church, like you said, the shit has hit the fan." A smile creased his face while remembering Butch's description of how Goldie had dropped like a rag doll.

"Our problem now is that Goldie is mad and unpredictable. Will he drop a dime with the cops, or will he try to take it to the streets against you? The smart move is the former. However, when you're thinking in anger, you tend to make mistakes. So, he'll probably do the latter."

George made the statement more to focus Churchill than to review the situation.

"So Church, first, take a big chill pill, a deep breath, and relax. Secondly, let's make plans to get you out of here. I've got the money from Connie, Romy and Liddy, which will get you to New York and then on a plane to San Antonio. When you get to San Antonio, cross the border at Laredo and make your way to Cozumel. Chill in Mexico for a month or two. I'll find you there."

Churchill immediately responded, "I'm not leaving without Ramona."

ଔଋଔ

Bauer realized now that the only thing that was going to get the pressure off of him was significant progress on the Black October case. Trey's arrest had diffused the initial pressure, but, like a bad penny, it was back. He had to get a better take on this thing. The only serious suspect was Goldie. Goldie made sense because of where Romy got knocked off. Maybe he was even smart enough to eliminate competition under the guise of an organization like Black October. He had to do something, and Goldie was it for the moment.

"I want to know what that motherfucking Goldie's doing every minute of every day," Bauer screamed across the office.

The news of Churchill's confrontation with Goldie swept through the Harlem Avenue neighborhood.

When Ramona heard the news, she dashed from the house, heading for the neighborhood gathering spot. It was empty with no sign of Churchill or Butch. As she walked back up Harlem Avenue, two men pulled alongside her in the gold Continental Mark IV.

"Hey, Ramona."

Ramona didn't recognize the men, and she immediately went on alert.

"Who wants to know?" she replied cautiously,

"Churchill sent us to get you and bring you along. He says he wants you off the streets right now."

Hearing Churchill's name, she questioned.

"Where's he at?"

The barrel of a pistol appeared, and it was pointed at her midsection.

"Be quiet and get in. You'll see him soon enough."

ଔଔଔ

Churchill and George worked on strategic approaches, taking each potential situation and dissecting its pros and cons and their reaction to each.

They were playing high-level street chess, and it was for all the marbles. George's focused intelligence and Churchill's strategic war and leadership skills honed their analyses as if they were in the Oval Office or the Pentagon.

Their concentration was broken by Butch's coded knock. As George let him in, Churchill immediately knew something was wrong.

"What?" he implored.

"They've taken Ramona, Church."

Churchill steamed for the front door, only to be blocked by George.

"No Church, they're trying to draw you out."

Churchill pushed by George knocking him down with ease, only to be grabbed by Butch.

"Stop, Church," they pleaded in unison.

ଔଔଔ

Commander Bauer listened to the voice on the other end of the line.

"Commander, we've been watching that dealer named Goldie and just saw the damnest thing."

"What?" inquired Bauer.

"You know that girl you've been interviewing about the Liddell murder?"

"Yeah, the one named Dee-Dee?" replied Bauer.

"Yeah sir, her, the pretty one. Anyway, I just saw her or her twin walk into Goldie's house with two of his men."

Bauer's mind screamed, *I knew it! It wasn't Dee-Dee I'd seen before. It was Romy's girlfriend. It all fit now. This girl or these girls were part of the set-up, and Goldie was behind it all. Either that or Goldie took out Romy to get his girl, which I could readily understand. He also took out Connie to take over his drug operation. Slick! It was Goldie all along.*

Goldie's telephone number had been on Romy's body, but I hadn't given it much credence at the time. This was going to be good. I can take out Goldie, killing two birds with one stone. I'll dump the Black October stuff on him and knock off a homicidal major dealer at the same time. The girls? Were they sisters, twins or what? Whatever, the ultimate prize could be one or both of the girls with me.

Bauer screamed, "Set up the war room, and get the task force ready. We've got some ass to kick."

಄಄಄

"Churchill, Churchill!" George yelled from the seat of his pants. "Stop, we didn't do all this planning for you to go flying out the door out of control."

No one was happier to hear George's words than Butch because his effort to hold Churchill left him beaten and exhausted.

Finally, Churchill said through sobs and tears, "I can't lose her, man. I just can't lose her."

The tears flowed in earnest, and George and Butch just looked at each other. They had never seen this side of Churchill before. They consoled him as best they could.

಄಄಄

Ramona walked into the row house and was initially shocked at its ambience. Her mind revolted, thinking, *Who lives here?*

On cue, Goldie stepped from behind a curtain of stranded multicolored beads.

"So, you Church's girl. You definitely fine, and I see why he into you. You was Romy's girl before dat too. Wasn't you?" Terror filled Ramona, and she knew instantly she was in deep trouble.

"You know who kilted Romy, don't you? It dat nigga you fucking now! Ain't it? Well, we'll find out what you know!"

The implication that Church was involved in Romy's murder

shocked Ramona, but a strength she never experienced welled up in her. She intuitively knew it was from her connection to Churchill. She looked at Goldie dabbing the cloth to his mouth and let out a small laugh.

"If you think you had a problem with Church before, I promise you ain't seen nothing yet. He will come for me."

Revealing his gap-toothed smile, Goldie said, "Dat's what I'm hoping for."

With eyes full of warning, Ramona replied, "Be careful what you ask for. You just may get it. Knowing Churchill like I do, you'll end up being more than just snaggletoothed."

Goldie sauntered toward Ramona, expecting her to retreat in fear, but her eyes stayed transfixed on him, showing no sign of backing down. Goldie stopped inches from her face and stared directly in her eyes.

"So you ain't scared of Goldie, huh? I ain't heard a bitch get smart wit me in a dog's age, but here you is." Goldie reached out and tore the front off of Ramona's blouse. Ramona fell back trying to cover her breasts.

೧೩೦೩೦೩

Bauer was ecstatic. Goldie was in his crosshairs, and he was going to pull the trigger. He had already informed the commissioner and selected elected officials that his target was Goldie, and the hammer was going to fall on Black October as soon as tonight.

೧೩೦೩೦೩

George had his hands on Churchill's shoulders while looking him straight in the eyes.

"Church, don't run out there in a rage. They have to send a message telling you where to come for Ramona. It's all just a set-up. We got to wait for the message, and pray for Ramona's safety. Stay on point here because whatever happens, you, Ramona, and Butch are going to end up in Mexico. Only now you're going to have to drive.

"Butch has the homeboys on alert, and they're scouring the

streets for Goldie. One way or another, they either find him, or we learn the spot for the set-up. We've got to cover one key point. I sent Butch to get the .38, the .45, and the flyers used in the executions. That's going to be our end game. My connections just informed me that the cops think Goldie's behind the whole Black October thing. If we play our cards right, we can come out of this smelling like a rose. So get yourself together and focused. We need our war general, and we need you now."

Goldie's inevitable message for a meeting was dropped off at Ramona's house in an envelope addressed to Churchill. When he, Butch, and George saw the sheet of paper, Churchill's face became a mask of fury, and even Butch could not look at him without shivers running up his back. Churchill cleaned his nails with a dagger he brought back from Vietnam, occasionally tossing it in the air to catch its hilt as George read from the letter.

"He wants to meet in Leakin Park by the football field." Churchill slowly nodded his head.

They find a lot of dead bodies in Leakin Park, and Goldie's going to be next.

"He says that only you Churchill and Butch come into the park. Once you're there, they'll release Ramona to Butch, but Church, you have to stay behind alone and unarmed."

Finishing the reading, George looked at Churchill's mask of fury and saw a calm come over him.

Churchill said, "Let's go." Before he could get up, George put a hand on his shoulder.

"Good luck. I have one more move to make, and the rest is on you, my brother. Bring Ramona back."

ଔଔଔ

Bauer was in his war room as his radiophone squealed.

"Commander Bauer, Goldie, and a bunch of his men are on the move, and they have the girl with them."

"Stay on them," barked Bauer.

However, Bauer was still puzzling over the anonymous telephone call telling them that Goldie was Black October, and he was going to knock off another dealer in Leakin Park tonight. They were on it, but the call was puzzling.

When it rains, it pours, he thought.

Churchill and Butch were dropped off on Franklintown Road and walked toward the football field in Leakin Park. They arrived ahead of Goldie, giving Churchill time to stash Black October flyers under a black cloth.

Churchill felt for the comfort of the .38 and .45 pistols in his waistband as he and Butch acclimated themselves to the environment. They were completely silent and focused on the sounds of the crickets. Their eyes adjusted to the pitch darkness by the intermittent illumination of lightning bugs. Time stood still, and both men became lost in their thoughts.

Headlights appeared in the distance, and a car edged to a stop. Churchill and Butch had positioned themselves with their backs to the football field, and they surveyed the Mark IV as it slowly headed in their direction. The situation was playing out as they hoped. They were sure that Goldie thought he was blocking the only way out of the park. From his football days, Churchill knew another path out of the park and had a car idling at the spot. He knew the face-off with Goldie was on him.

Goldie stepped from the car surveying the scene. Seeing only Churchill and Butch, he smiled. He reached into the car and roughly snatched Ramona by the neck, shoving her hard against the car beside him. Three other figures moved from the car into the night. Churchill's eyes narrowed and focused on Ramona. Even through the darkness, he could see her clothing was torn and disheveled

"Be cool Church. Be cool. At least four rods out there," Butch pleaded.

Churchill was motionless, his eyes like a lion's blazing into the darkness. Goldie pimped toward them, one hand at the back of Ramona's neck and the other with a pistol hanging at his side. As he approached, he said, "Looks like we meet again, Church."

"Let her go!" came the fierce command from Churchill.

Goldie's golden smile showed a large black gap in the middle.

"You can have dis bitch now. I'm done. The pussy's good, but this skank couldn't make my stable."

"Let her go," Churchill commanded again pulling the .38 and .45 from his waistband with gloved hands.

"Now, now, Church, they ain't the rules we gonna play by. First, you drop the heat, and then I let her go."

Churchill replied, "Let her walk to my man, and I'll put the guns at my feet and step back. When they're moving out of the park, I'll kick the guns to you."

"Awright," Goldie shot back. "That'll work, but if you make any kinda crazy move, I'll blow this bitch away," he said while roughly shoving Ramona forward.

Ramona stumbled, pulling her clothes around her. As she moved forward, Churchill slowly knelt, placing the pistols on the ground in front of him.

"Get to Butch, now!" he barked as Ramona started toward him.

"Goldie, my man is packing heavy heat. Let him and Ramona go, and you'll have just me," Churchill offered in a conciliatory manner.

"Dat's what I want Church. Dat's what I want," Goldie replied, his face twisting into a sinister sneer.

His reputation had been damaged, and he planned to repair it tonight. When Ramona reached Butch, Goldie assumed they had to walk toward him, and he'd get them right after Churchill. To his surprise, they darted to Churchill's rear, disappearing into the darkness.

Alarmed, he immediately leveled his gun at Churchill, who raised his hands. Goldie quickly became comfortable with his gun on Churchill and the three men at his back.

"Pull up your shirt, Church," Goldie commanded.

Churchill complied as Goldie sauntered toward him. Goldie's men closed quickly on his flanks and rear in support.

Ten feet away from Churchill, Goldie, said, "You gonna knock out my teeth and think you're going to get away wit it, huh? This is the night the bad-ass Churchill meets his maker. I just got one question motherfucker, and you may as well answer truthfully because your ass is dead. Was you behind all this Black October shit?"

"Yeah," replied Churchill defiantly, "and I only made one mistake."

"What was that dead man?" Goldie smiled.

"I should have killed you first."

"I tell you what, Church. Back away from those guns!"

Churchill did as he was instructed.

Goldie picked up the .38 and tossed it aside. He kept the .45 in his empty hand. He approached Churchill while tasting the blood from between his displaced teeth.

Churchill didn't fear Goldie's approach but thought, *Georgie, I need your miracle now. Just give me a chance to make him pay for messing with Ramona.*

Looking at Goldie, Churchill yelled, "Here, maybe you want these too!"

He kicked a stack of Black October flyers into the air. The flyers went into the air and scattered about.

"You is a real funny motherfucker, Church, and you're also a dead motherfucker, but we're going to blow you apart one shot at a time."

Goldie waved the pistols in the air.

"I don't know what all dis paper about. I know it ain't gonna save yo' ass!"

"Hey Goldie, what you call a motherfucker with his front teeth knocked out?"

"Awright funny guy, what?

"A punk motherfucker!"

Goldie leveled both pistols at Churchill.

"You're dead!"

As soon as the words were out of Goldie's mouth, floodlights illuminated the night, and a megaphone blared.

"This is the Baltimore City Police Department. Put down your weapons, and put your hands in the air."

Goldie turned to the source of the light and sound saying, "Shit!"

Immediately turning back, he felt Churchill on him.

Churchill stepped to Goldie's right side, breaking his right wrist and disarming him. Goldie got off a wild shot with the .45 as Churchill fractured his neck. He simultaneously spun the body between himself and Goldie's men. They started shooting wildly, and two bullets thudded into Goldie's chest as Churchill used him as a human shield.

The shots started an all-out police onslaught.

Goldie's men fell under the police fire and were soon dead. Churchill retreated backwards continuing to use Goldie as a shield.

Once he was away from the police floodlights, he dropped Goldie's body and fell to the ground, crawling as fast as he could. He covered more yards than he could count before jumping up and sprinting through the pitch-black night.

⊗⊗⊗

The next day, the police commissioner, the mayor, and Commander Bauer were at the podium in front of City Hall for their press conference.

The mayor spoke first.

"Thanks to the sustained and diligent efforts of the commissioner, Commander Bauer, and our police department, the clandestine organization known as Black October was dealt a severe blow last night. Four members of Black October were killed in a shootout with police. At the scene, the guns used to kill Connie Gordon, Romeo Mason, and Sam Liddell were recovered along with Black October documents. We are confident that the main culprits behind Black October have been eliminated."

Bauer smiled as he thought, *I wonder who broke Goldie's wrist and neck. And what happened to that girl?*

CHAPTER SEVENTEEN

"And affords the traveler his love, children, life and soul."

As Judge Abrams provided instructions to the jury, Trey suppressed a smug grin.

Boy, did I get lucky closing last. It was more dumb luck than anything. He could see Gosselin seething knowing he'd been outfoxed.

Now the closing is upon me, and it's a make-or-break situation. The preponderance of evidence rests with the prosecution, and the difference has to be made here.

Judge Abrams broke Trey's thoughts.

"Mr. Ballard, are you ready to make your closing argument?"

Trey replied quickly, "May I have five minutes, Your Honor?" Trey bent over the notes in front of him and prayed for deliverance. He prayed for Candace, his mother, and the Right Reverend. He felt their collective strength flood his being. But he needed to finish his own mental journey.

ೲೞೲ

Trey thought back to the night of the riot at Lorton and the last time he saw Tony and Scar.

Trey heard Scar scream, "Tony!"

Tony turned in his tracks, eyes blazing into Scar. Trey couldn't quite tell if the blaze in his eyes were a reflection from the fire or hate blazing from within.

Scar bellowed, "I been wanting you since you put this beauty mark on my face, and you're paying for it tonight!"

Tony slowly replied, his voice rising from his gut, "I've been running too long Little Bit. I'm tired of your shit, and I was never scared of you in the first place."

Chiseled muscle had grown on both men over the years, and their appearances had changed greatly from the two boys who had fought almost a decade earlier.

Tony was tall and bronze with a sprinter's physique. Scar was blue-black, medium height, and heavy-set. He was not an ugly man, but his hate-filled life would not allow his beauty to show through. They walked to each other with measured paces reminiscent of a high-noon showdown. Their paces slowed as the distance closed, and their eyes narrowed while sizing each other up.

Trey raced between them screaming, "No, no, no!"

"Stay outta dis, Trey" hissed Scar in a voice barely audible but with the intent of stopping Trey in his tracks.

Tony said succinctly, not taking his blazing eyes off of Scar, "This is overdue. You're outta this, Trey."

Trey drew his breath and exhaled slowly as he stepped back and to the side. He gritted his teeth and raised his head to the sky for deliverance. His body shook while trying to think of a way to stop the confrontation. Suddenly and to his dismay he realized, *This was a fight to the death.*

The two men paused as they reached striking distance, sharing an icicle-laden stare. They slowly began to circle, putting their arms in the on-guard position. Tony initiated a slow Muhammad Ali-like shuffle while Scar crouched lower, bending his back and jutting his head forward between his guards.

Tony advanced quickly, starting the combat with a stiff left jab to Scar's face and following it with a vicious right cross to his jaw, knocking Scar off balance and two steps to the right. The right cross would have knocked out most men, but the anger and hate within Scar made him shake it off like a bee sting.

Tony fired another series of punches, with Scar absorbing, ducking, or blocking them. Tony faked another left jab and sent a vicious right cross like the first, but Scar grabbed his arm, spun, and stepped backwards inside of Tony, pulling his arm down hard over his shoulder. The move bent Tony's arm hideously. Stepping further back into Tony, Scar slammed the crown of his head up and into Tony's chin. The tooth-rattling blow sent Tony's head snapping back and him reeling to the floor.

Tony shook his head to clear the cobwebs and grabbed at his arm and shoulder feeling for damage, but Scar was already on the attack, leaping on him and trying to pin him to the floor. Tony countered the attack with an open-handed blast into Scar's solar plexus and then used both feet to kick him off. Falling back, Scar hesitated and then dove headfirst at Tony. Tony elevated his feet into Scar's stomach, executing a perfect monkey flip. Scar landed heavily on his back and grunted as air escaped from his lungs.

Tony was quickly on his feet but staggering backward as he continued to feel and work on his arm and shoulder. Scar rose from the ground and smiled as he pulled a four-inch, homemade knife from his pant leg. Gasping for breath, he said, "Tony, the scar I leave on you is going to end up spilling your guts."

Tony continued retreating and massaging his arm and shoulder. Scar advanced in a crouching stance with the knife extended in front of him. To Trey's surprise, he saw flickering lights reflecting on the knife's blade. The revelation broke Trey's concentration on the fight and made him look up and around.

Through the window, Trey could see fires raging out of control. The bright red and yellow flames twenty to thirty feet high burned above Lorton's Occoquan I and II dormitories. Fires had burned through the roofs of some buildings and ignited large sections of the courtyard, including the catwalk areas. He now realized the catwalks would be a good escape route.

His mind jetted between the escape potential and the fight. He was stuck in a trance-like state, not knowing whether to escape or watch the fight. And then his head whipped back to the fight.

Scar was advancing on Tony, flicking the blade at him. Tony was sidestepping Scar's feints, jumping back and to the side. Even though the room was large, Tony had retreated to a far corner. Trey couldn't tell if it were a strategic retreat or whether Scar's knife-wielding skills had forced him into the corner.

Panicked, Tony peered over his shoulder at the wall trapping him in the corner. He winced as his arm and shoulder seemed to drop helplessly to his side. Suddenly, Tony made a guttural sound and charged Scar, reaching to grab the wrist wielding the knife. Adeptly avoiding Tony's grab, Scar countered and just missed sinking the blade deep into Tony's stomach. Tony's quickness was the only thing that saved him from the deadly thrust.

Scar began a steadier advance with Tony's head jetting side to side, looking for a weapon of his own. Trey felt totally helpless. He didn't want this, but this showdown was inevitable. The fight wasn't fair, and they were both his friends. Trey decided that Tony needed a fair chance, and he needed to do something to even the fight or stop it.

Before he could do anything, Tony and Scar were wrestling for the knife. Tony now had his back to Scar with the knife in front of him. Scar was trying to force the blade into Tony's torso. Then Tony sidestepped, turned, and whipped the blade backwards and deep into Scar's stomach. Tony finished his spinning move with a crescent kick to the back of Scar's neck forcing him to fall onto the blade.

Scar cried out in pain as the blade pushed through to his spine. He rolled off the blade and writhed from side-to-side, clutching the blade and his stomach. A gurgling sound and a tortured whisper left his lips. Then he was motionless. In an instant, he was Little Bit again. Tony stood over Scar in a Tarzan-like triumphant stance. Trey almost expected him to beat his chest and let out Tarzan's scream.

Trey raced quickly to Tony's side.

"Tony, you've got to get out of here. You know Scar's boys are going to kill you now. You've got to escape, and there's no better time than now. The catwalks are on fire, and I think you can get through."

"Let's go then," Tony responded while looking down at Scar's lifeless body and the embedded knife.

"No Tony," Trey responded sadly.

Tony looked into Trey's eyes.

"What are you saying, man? We gotta get outta here and now."

"Tony, like you I'm tired of running. I've got to stay and fight my way out of this place."

Tony looked at Trey and winced in pain. He used one arm to pull him into a hug and whispered, "I love you man."

"You gotta go, Tony, if anybody can get outta here, you can. Find Churchill, he'll help you. Just tell him I sent you."

Tony smiled, pushed Trey away, spun, and dashed into the

night. He disappeared, seemingly devoured by the darkness and flame. It reminded Trey of Tony's narrow escape from Scar and his compatriots in Evergreen Park. He strained his eyes to watch as his friend disappeared from sight. Trey looked down at Scar's body and said, "Damn, why?"

༶༶༶

The thoughts of the events that led Trey to this juncture in his life dissipated. He felt whole for the first time in many years. A weight seemed to lift from his shoulders as he looked around the courtroom. He smiled with the anticipation of defending and freeing himself. Judge Abrams again broke Trey's thoughts, her irritation evident as her voice rose an octave.

"Mr. Ballard, are you ready to proceed?"

Trey rose from his chair immaculately dressed in his blue pinstriped suit. The suit was accessorized with a red paisley necktie and white, buttoned-down shirt. He cleared his throat and coughed before speaking in a tone of strength and defiance.

"Yes, Your Honor, I am ready to proceed."

He nodded his head respectfully to the judge, jury, and slightly to the prosecution table. He turned and looked lovingly at his parents who had aged considerably, making him wince. Trey smiled broadly and bent slightly from the waist to each. He poured a drink of water and took several gulps. He'd seen his father pause for effect hundreds of times in church and followed suit now.

Just as Judge Abrams was ready to admonish him for the delay, he began.

"Ladies and gentlemen of the jury, I stand before you today in defense of myself and my future." He eased forward to the jury box and gently looked into the eyes of each member.

"I am charged with conspiracy to riot and arson at Lorton. Those charges are felonies and federal offenses.

"I have presented witnesses who have testified under oath that I did not encourage anyone to riot, nor did I start any fires. They testified that I tried to dissuade any thought of violence. Yes, I knew there were plans to create a disturbance, and technically, I should have reported that to the authorities."

Trey paused but finished quickly, his tone animated, "However that is not what I am charged with.

"Let's take that a step further. Suppose I did report plans about a proposed disturbance. How long do you think that I, an informant, would have survived inside the walls of Lorton?"

After pausing for effect he continued, his voice rose.

"I'll tell you, not long, and my life would not have been worth a plugged nickel."

He hesitated and strode to the prosecution table. He waved his hand in the direction of Gosselin and his seconds saying. "The learned prosecutor, Mr. Gosselin, has been very forceful and correct in pointing out the problems inside Lorton Reformatory."

Emphasizing each word, he looked at the jury.

"If Mr. Gosselin, the federal, state, and prison authorities can't control the environment," he again paused placing fingers on his chest, "how do they expect me to do it?" He started again with his voice reaching a crescendo, "And do it under a sentence of death from my fellow inmates!"

Trey slowly walked back to the jury box shaking his hung head.

He lifted his head as he reached the box, surveyed the jury, and continued. "Why am I here in front of you? I'm arguing for a chance to get my life back. I want to be a son to my mother and father. I want to be a husband to the woman I love and father to our children."

Trey extended his arms palms up, continuing.

"Those are the reasons I must succeed today." His eyes were wide and candid.

"I could not leave my life and future in someone else's hands. They are far too important to me and to my loved ones."

Placing the fingers from his left hand on his chest and addressing the jury, he animated his voice.

"Who knows my life and circumstance better than I? Yes, I am an inmate. Should I be in jail? No."

Trey stopped and let the word hang in the air.

"No," he repeated again more forcefully.

He let the courtroom become completely silent before he continued.

"Ladies and gentlemen of the jury, I shouldn't be in jail. Five years ago, the Baltimore City Police Department shot and killed four drug dealers and murderers and then proclaimed they were the men who committed the crimes I'm in jail for now."

He paused for effect again.

"Maybe you remember the case associated with the murder of the Maryland Delegate James Gordon and the group called Black October? I'm supposed to be Black October," he said while thrusting his hands in the air and staggering backward feigning shock.

"At the time, I was a student going into my junior year at Howard University. Did I have a connection to Black October or the murderers or the drug dealers? No," he emphasized the word, and let it hang in the air.

Starting slowly and leaning into the jury box, he continued.

"Please understand," he paused, "that I have a great chance at being granted an appeal and having my original conviction overturned. If that is the case, then where's my motive and motivation for participating in events that would prolong or even cement my incarceration? I don't see it. Do you?"

"Yes, I heard plans for the demonstration, and I argued for the forum we are standing in now to take up the challenge. I've always believed that the pen is mightier than the sword. I do not believe in destruction, violence, or chaos. I set fire to nothing, and I encouraged no one to riot or even tear a single brick from Lorton's foundation."

Trey moved so that he stood an equal distance between the judge and jury and alternately addressed both as he continued.

"Instead, I pleaded for sanity and safety. I asked that grievances be brought in front of a judge and jury like you. And, I prayed that they would be just, honest, and had the God-given instincts to know right from wrong. I ask you to be that type of jury today and free me from these charges."

Savoring his words and speaking in a low tone, he said, "If I am freed from these charges, there is a chance I will be released from prison, a chance I can go home to my family"

Trey strode in the direction of the Right Reverend and his mother. The passion in his voice grew, and he became teary-eyed. He spoke in a very low tone, and his voice cracked to a degree.

"There is a chance that," he breathed deeply, his chest expanding and contracting greatly, "that I will be reunited with the woman I love."

Trey wiped at his eyes and felt the presence of tears. "There is a chance I will go back to school and get my law degree and stand before you as a member of the bar, instead of an unjustly imprisoned man fighting for his life and future."

Trey moved back to the jury.

"Today, I ask you to give me those chances and my God-given rights to life, liberty, and the pursuit of happiness. I guarantee you will not be disappointed with the result."

Trey looked at the jury for several moments and finally stated, "Thank you, ladies and gentlemen of the jury." He turned to the bench and nodded.

"Thank you, Your Honor."

As Trey strode back to his chair, he watched as the Right Reverend rose and silently applauded.

03CS03

Dedication/Acknowledgments

"It is our destiny and our choice."

The writing of this book has been a labor of love and a cathartic experience for this author. It is written with love and as a memoir for my beautiful and talented son, Jamal; his sisters Aasia and Cortney; and my grandsons, Jahkai and Jamal Jr. It is hoped that this book will serve as a protector to them and contribute to their living a life of pride, dignity, and courage.

The book is dedicated in loving memory to my mother, Albertha, and my father, John Archer Crawley, Jr. Albertha was a woman of incredible strength and courage. Her beauty, power, and gifts of tough love will forever be appreciated. My father was one of the greatest men I have ever known. I admire no man more. It is hoped that my son and grandsons understand the male relationships expressed in this book.

Special thanks for the love, insight, and encouragement of my family and friends: my brothers, Clinton, Joe, Jason, and Jeffrey; my sisters, Barbara, Neicy, Gwen, Wanda, and Vikki; my brethren, Carlton, James Daniel, Dino, Gary, Bobby, and George; and my elders, Emma, Margaret, Charles, Joe, Mary, Fannie, Rufus, Sarah, Harper, Betty, Lee, Charlie, and Sadie — who are with or looking down on us.

Lastly, this book is written in memory of Black October. The actions of its members were predicated on a love of their people and desire to combat the scourge of drugs. Hopefully, this small treatise will record their place in history.

This author does not consider himself a racist and the terminology used in this book should not be misconstrued as an attack on any race, color, or creed. Certain dialogue was necessary to reflect the exact sentiments of the times and portray events in their best literary sense. This author abhors racism in all its manifestations. I trust readers will take this story to heart and then look into their hearts to find a way to destroy this insidious disease.

As a famous musical group once said, "America Eats Its

Young." If this book can help eradicate the kind of thinking that contributes to racism, drug abuse, and the destruction of America's youth, it has been well worth this author's time and energy.